LAST OF HER NAME

LAST OF
HER NAME

A NOVELLA & STORIES

MIMI LOK

KAYA PRESS

Printed in the United States

22   21   20   19   4   3   2   1

Published by Kaya Press
kaya.com

Distributed by D.A.P. / Distributed Art Publishers
artbook.com / (800) 388-BOOK
ISBN: 978-1-885030-61-0

Library of Congress Control Number: 2019941897

Cover artwork by Seonna Hong
Cover and book design by Sunra Thompson

Earlier versions of these stories have appeared in the following publications:
McSweeney's Quarterly, *Nimrod International Journal of Prose and Poetry*, and *Hyphen*.

This publication is made possible by support from the USC Dana and David Dornsife
College of Arts, Letters, and Sciences; the Shinso Ito Center for Japanese Religions and
Culture; and the USC Department of American Studies and Ethnicity. Special thanks to the
Choi Chang Soo Foundation for their support of this work.

Additional funding was provided by the generous contributions of: Christine Alberto, Tiffany
Babb, Manibha Banerjee, Tom and Lily So Beischer, Piyali Bhattacharya, Anelise Chen, Anita
Chen, Lisa Chen, Floyd Cheung, Jen Chou, Kavita Das, Steven Doi, Susannah Donahue, Jessica
Eng, Sesshu Foster, Jean Ho, Heidi Hong, Huy Hong, Jayson Joseph, Sabrina Ko, Juliana Koo,
Whakyung Lee, Andrew Leong, Edward Lin, Leza Lowitz, Edan Lepucki, Faisal Mohyuddin,
Nayomi Munaweera, Abir Majumdar, Viet Thanh Nguyen, Sandra Noel, Yun and Minkyung Oh,
Chez Bryan Ong, Gene & Sabine Oishi, Leena Pendharker, Eming Piansay, Amarnath Ravva,
Andrew Shih, Paul H. Smith, Shinae Yoon, Monona Wali, Patricia Wakida, Duncan Williams,
Amelia Wu & Sachin Adarkar, Anita Wu & James Spicer, Koon Woon, Mikoto Yoshida, Nancy
Yap, Patricia and Andy Yun, and others.

Kaya Press is also supported in part by the National Endowment for the Arts; the Los Angeles
County Board of Supervisors through the Los Angeles County Arts Commission; the City of Los
Angeles Department of Cultural Affairs; and the Community of Literary Magazines and Presses.

For my family and all of my *sifus* along the way

CONTENTS

LAST OF HER NAME

AT AGE TWELVE KAREN knocks her teeth out. Lying in a stiff, tangled heap on the bedroom floor, she opens her mouth to let the blood seep out, and with her tongue she feels one, two, three holes where her teeth used to be. She quietly marvels at the wreckage she's created: the wardrobe, planted face down on the floor; the rug, splattered with blood and mirror shards; the limp, frayed coil of the skipping rope poking out from the rubble of upturned books and cushions.

Moments earlier, Karen had tied one end of the rope to the door and the other end to the wardrobe in an attempt to recreate a scene from *The Return of the Condor Heroes*, her favorite mou hap TV show. In this scene, the heroine Dragon Girl demonstrates her skill by sleeping on a single rope suspended four feet above the ground, the hem of her white robes grazing the floor with each soft exhalation. It seemed so effortless, so elegant. How was Karen supposed to know that her slight ninety-pound self would be enough to send the wardrobe crashing to the floor?

Looking up at the ceiling, Karen strains to wiggle her fingers and toes. They feel thick and dull, as if wrapped in cotton wool, but at least she can feel them. She imagines her mother standing in the doorway, stunned into silence by the tableau of destruction before her eyes, then coming to her senses and rushing to her side so she can begin checking for wounds, tut-tutting all the while at this display of foolishness. Karen hopes she will somehow realize that her daughter can't possibly be solely to blame for this mishap. Her poor father, perhaps, will be faulted for renting the mou hap videos in the first place—pirated recordings of Hong Kong shows that are delivered to their house each Saturday morning. Karen knows her mother considers this an extravagance, especially since the driver charges extra for coming all the way out to the suburbs from Chinatown. But with any luck, some of her mother's ire will be directed at Karen's younger sister Maria. Every weekend, the girls act out fight scenes from *The Return of the Condor Heroes*, running around the garden and swinging broom handles at each other, landing kicks and punches while their mother occasionally looks up from her weeding to shout, "Avoid the head!" (She doesn't mind so much that they hit each other but insists that they avoid brain damage.) At first, the sisters would toss a coin for the coveted part of Dragon Girl, who was beautiful and heroic and could boast the best weapons: an army of jade bees commanded with a series of whistles; poisonous needles used as deadly projectiles; and a long sash that shot out from her waist to attack an opponent's pressure points in both long- and short-range attacks. But Maria soon monopolized the role of Dragon Girl by refusing to play unless she was guaranteed the part, forcing Karen, unwilling to lose her only collaborator, to accept the villainous role of the Scarlett Immortal. The signature weapon of the Scarlett Immortal, a man-hating Taoist nun, was a flywhisk, a ridiculous-looking object that resembled a giant brush. Surely her mother would be able to see the injustice that had set her on the path to this ill-advised endeavor?

But to Karen's surprise, her mother doesn't tut-tut when she sees the mess in the bedroom. She doesn't demand an explanation or reel off a list of culprits. She simply sweeps her hands slowly over her injured daughter and proceeds to lightly press her fingers along her body, checking for breaks, sprains, cuts. Years later, Karen will think back to this moment—her mother, squatting down beside her, her face darkened. But right now, all that Karen knows is her fear that her mother's silence is somehow connected to the severity of the injuries.

"Silly girl," says her mother. Karen detects an unfamiliar trembling in her voice. "You should know it's not real."

"What do you mean, 'it's not real'?" asks Maria, peering in from the doorway.

"Telephone," says their mother, one hand outstretched, the other smoothing strands of hair from Karen's bloody forehead. She dials 999 and says in her staccato English, "Ambulance please! June Leung, 5 Clover Hill. Accident, bad fall. No, not me! My daughter."

Karen loses two incisors and a molar and a little dignity. She gains a fat, pink neck brace and a swollen cheek covered with purple and yellow blooms. Maria hangs off the hospital bed frame with her gymnast's arms, alternating her hands.

"I can't believe you were that stupid," she giggles. "Pretending to be Dragon Girl. Sleeping on a *rope*. Hahaha!"

Karen's face hurts too much to scowl. But she is consoled by the doctor's recommendation of home rest for a week, perhaps even two. That's potentially two weeks off from school.

Out in the hall, Karen's mother and father talk about the restaurant being shorthanded that week.

"I can still cover the lunch shift tomorrow," says her mother. "She'll be mostly sleeping anyway."

"No, Jun-Jun, they can manage," says her father, "Our little girl's had a scare. We should both stay with her, at least for a day or two."

"Ah Tin, you spoil her."

"We have to take care of our girls."

"Maria wouldn't be this careless."

Jun-Jun. Ah Tin. Karen's parents reserve the use of their Chinese names for private debate over the girls, the business, the house, as well as for moments of intimacy—Karen knows this from years of pressing her ear against closed doors. They use their English names, June and Stanley, when speaking with English people, or when they have to fill out a form. In front of the girls, they address each other by their title or function—"Wife/Husband" or "Mother/Father." Sometimes Karen observes these frequent transpositions without much thought beyond a vague admiration for her parents' talent for adaptability. At other times—when a customer nonchalantly says "chink" in the restaurant they own or a neighbor peers over the garden fence as her father snaps the neck of a chicken—she feels a brief, nauseating unease at these interchangeable guises and how they might suggest to others that her parents are not actually who they say they are, resulting in some dreadful punishment.

But right now, lying in the hospital bed, Karen doesn't care about any of this. She's just thinking, *Two weeks off school!* She'll have to keep up a bit with homework, her mother will see to that. But otherwise she can just stay home and spend her days watching *mou hap* videos. She prays for this to be true to whoever might be listening: the goddess of mercy, the god of war, the goddess of the sea, the god of fortune, the goddess of the moon, Jesus, the Dragon Girl and her army of bees. Even the Scarlett Immortal.

HONG KONG, 1941

The Japanese army is preparing to launch their attack, and the idiot boy is kicking Jun-Jun in the legs.

"Ha!" He kicks her again and again. "Ha! Ha!" He whirls around like a malfunctioning spinning top, tracing an erratic path around the concrete front yard that also serves as a thoroughfare for the village. He almost knocks the hat off a farmer steering his ox towards the fields. The farmer catches his hat with a startled laugh and nods at Great Uncle Chutt as if to say, *No harm done.*

Jun-Jun maintains the jak ma drill position: eyes forward; palms centered; knees bent.

"Try again, try to knock her over!" says Great Uncle Chutt.

The boy, laughing, pushes himself against her legs, punches her arms, and tickles her sides. Jun-Jun imagines high-kicking him to the other side of the fields. He calls her *Je Je*—big sister.

He'd wandered into the village square ten days before, ragged, dirty, and malnourished, making odd, hooting sounds and chuckling to himself incessantly. Great Uncle Chutt took pity on him and pulled him away from the laughing faces. He gave the boy a bowl of rice with a piece of salted fish, which he ate on the stone ground with his hands. When he finished, the boy licked the bowl inside and out, which made Great Uncle Chutt slap his thigh and whistle his approval. Jun-Jun knew then that she'd never get rid of him.

"Had enough, Jun-Jun?" Great Uncle Chutt's chicken-scratch voice makes her ears itch. "Had enough?" he repeats.

His lips smack-smack against the mouth of his pipe. At his feet, the tip of his cane stirs loose gravel, ocean waves to Jun-Jun's sensitive ears. *I hear you, Sifu,* thinks Jun-Jun. *You insult me, Sifu. I know this trick.* Has she not practiced tirelessly? Did she not prove herself on her first day of instruction, holding the jak ma position for a solid hour at age four? Has he forgotten all she has accomplished since that first day? By the age of six she could leap and trap a sparrow in her cupped hands. At nine she had mastered the pole form. At ten she'd driven her fist through a bench and left the skin on her knuckles intact. And yet, on this particular morning, she has been instructed to practice jak ma as if she were a novice.

Over the years she's become accustomed to Great Uncle Chutt's punishments, which usually consist of endlessly repeating a newly learned sequence or skill. She doesn't openly question or challenge him; for as long as she can remember, he has been her sole guardian, her teacher. There is also pride. She wants him to see that she can take all the punishments, expects them even. But nothing so basic as jak ma! She cannot think what she has done to upset him. She has always been diligent and humble. She hasn't been guilty of manifesting pride, which, to her Great Uncle Chutt, would give the greatest offense. But in her fury she thinks, *I can leap above your head, old man.* Great Uncle Chutt hobbles around her, examining her stance, and she's suddenly unnerved by the possibility that he can hear her thoughts. He grunts approval at the straightness of her back, the equilibrium of her centered palms. He turns to the boy.

"Try again," he instructs.

"Yes! Yes!"

The boy jumps up and down in front of her, beaming; he has fewer good teeth than the old man. The boy runs at her, lunging head first into her stomach. Jun-Jun is as solid as a tree, and the impact sends him back, wobbling one, two, three steps. She keeps her eyes forward; her skin is warm with fury. *Heavens*, thinks Jun-Jun. *Can you hear me? What will deliver me from this misery?*

Great Uncle Chutt is nodding, nodding.

"Again," he tells the boy.

ENGLAND, 1970

I can't live here, thinks June. Clover Hill. She's never been to this part of town before: leafy, manicured, and quiet. Why are there tiny pebbles on the front of that house? Why is there a hedge cut into the shape of a duck, or is it meant to be a chicken? And she's never seen a cul-de-sac before, let alone a cul-de-sac on a slope. It looks to her as if some higher power has slid a finger under the earth and tilted the landscape so that one terraced row stands considerably higher than the other. Can't her husband see that with their house on the top row, all their good fortune will drain away?

Yes, they're lucky to have got off the waiting list so soon. Yes, she should be grateful. But what, she wants to know, is the hurry? Can't they wait another year, if only to get a better deal? "It'll give a bad impression, Jun-Jun," explains her husband. "Remember what the lady from the housing office said? If we don't take a council house when we're offered one, they'll think we don't need it as much as everyone else. They might not even let us back on the waiting list." He takes her hand. "I know it doesn't look like much, but you'll see."

She knows he's trying his best. And she knows he's a good man, though she feared early on that she'd made a mistake. He'd left for England a few months after their wedding, following in the steps of countless men seeking better prospects overseas, and she'd expected him to forget her and take up with a young Englishwoman. But he'd sent her a letter each month with reports on his health, the weather, and his living and working conditions. He always included bank notes wrapped in butcher paper, even when he was between waiter jobs. He'd write, "Thank you for your patience, dear Jun-Jun. I am working hard to prepare a good situation for your arrival." She told him she didn't need the money, as she had her own income from the hair salon. But he'd insisted, and she'd dutifully relented, understanding that it was for him a matter of pride, and to some extent consolation, for failing to send for his wife in a timely manner.

She spent years waiting for him. During that time, she found that the more she imagined his perseverance in squalor, the more noble he seemed. And the more vindicated she felt in her decision to invest in this man of rare humility. She imagined his dingy bedsit, riddled with mold and cockroaches, and the floorboard under which he'd secrete money from his week's wages in a biscuit tin, saving towards their reunion fund. She imagined his cold, lonely nights in the restaurant basement, hunched over metal pails of potatoes as he scraped their skins off one by one, practicing the English phrases ("Good evening, Sir, Madam" "Have you made a reservation?" "I would recommend the lobster") that would get him out of the basement and secure a front-of-house position. All of it was for their future together.

Eventually Jun-Jun's wait was over. She stepped onto a plane for the very first time, clutching a handbag that contained her papers, her passport (complete with her new name, "June Leung," chosen by her husband), and, carefully folded between sheets of tissue paper, an embroidered picture she'd bought of two cranes perched on a treetop that symbolized matrimonial happiness.

"That wall," says June, pointing to the fat strip of road between two rows of houses that abruptly stops at a brick wall. "It's blocking the chi."

"Chi is important," says her husband, scratching his chin. "What if we sneak back here tonight and knock it down?"

"Very funny."

"This will be good for us," assures her husband. He gently pats her belly. "For all of us."

June discovers that she doesn't like to eat alone in this country. Stanley is at the restaurant most evenings, and although she tries to wait for him, being pregnant makes keen demands on her appetite. She's still getting used to their new cul-de-sac home; the quiet doesn't really agree with her. Eating her dinner in the silent, too-bright kitchen, she becomes almost wistful for their first home: a cramped, one-bedroom flat in the High Street.

The noise of the street and the smell of grease from the chip shop downstairs had made it easier to pretend she was back in Kowloon City, with its maze of neon ladders and the reassurance of dense, close-moving bodies.

On such evenings, June paces through the rooms of their new home, trying to reconcile herself to the previous tenants' taste. They've left a few pieces of furniture, most notably the wide, fifties-style drinks cabinet that she envisions as a possible shoe closet. Mostly, though, it's a virgin shell: rickety window frames that bone-rattle through the night; dark, grubby wallpaper the color of dry lichen; and a peeling orange slab of a front door with a knobby glass pane that tells you if someone is hovering behind it.

ENGLAND, 1983

Soon after she returns to school, Karen notices Ricky Stokes from Year Ten has started hanging around the auditorium entrance after her Monday and Wednesday choir practice. As she heads out of the hall with the other students, he calls out, "Where are you going?" or "Say hello." At first Karen doesn't realize he's talking to her. But then he starts saying her name in a coaxing, sing-song way, as if calling a lost dog. "Kaaaaaa-ren. Come on, give me a smile, Kaaaaren." She hurries past with her chin pressing into her neck brace, her mouth clamped firmly shut to hide her missing teeth, dismayed and surprised that he knows she exists.

She manages to avoid him during the day, ducking behind a corner when she catches sight of him. Like most of the Year Tens, Ricky Stokes looms over the younger students, but what makes him easier to pick out is the stark contrast between his pasty white face and his dark, spiky brush of hair. That plus his habit of loitering in the same spots at lunchtime—on the back steps of the auditorium or by the bike sheds—to smoke, or to fidget with his lighter or whatever object of interest he's picked up off the ground.

This continues for several weeks until one day, Ricky Stokes does not call out to Karen. Instead he follows her out of the school gate, trailing at first a few feet behind, then jogging ahead so that he's at her side. He asks her why she won't talk to him after all this time, does she think she's too good? Karen is alarmed by the accusation; she doesn't think she's better than anybody. She's a middling student, not popular like pretty, athletic Kerry Davies, or delicate and revered like Elaine Lally with the hole in her heart, or even intimidatingly aloof like Lois Meadows, pale and scowling under her tightly knotted headscarf. And she certainly can't boast of notoriety like Ricky Stokes, whose name is only ever mentioned in connection with some reckless misdeed or scandalous tragedy: a father in prison, an alcoholic mother and the string of unsuitable men she brought into her home, one of whom, Karen once heard a teacher say, knocked a five-year-old Ricky down the stairs during an argument with his mother.

Karen hunches her shoulders and keeps walking, suspecting that nothing she says will be the right answer. But her silence brings more questions:

"Why are you ignoring me? Are you deaf or something?"

She's trying to be clever, zig-zagging her route home through side streets and footpaths to throw him off her trail, but in her panic she leads them onto a too-quiet street, and by now it's almost dusk. There seems to be no one around except an elderly woman wheeling her shopping trolley up the steps to her front door. Karen calls to her, "Hello? Would you like some help?" but the woman shoots her a wary look and hurriedly closes the door behind her.

"You don't live here," says Ricky Stokes. There's an amused satisfaction in the statement, as if he's discovered the answer to a riddle, and before Karen can answer, he's grabbed her arm and is pushing her down a footpath behind the houses.

Later, when she thinks back to this moment, she won't remember much, only fragments. She'll remember the ground softening beneath her, tarmac turning to muddy grass, and that he'd somehow got his arm around her neck, his hand covering her face, his fingers smelling of cigarettes and other freshly burnt things— hair, skin, plastic. She'll remember her surprise at waking up in sudden darkness and thinking at first there was something wrong with her eyes; how she'd wondered how many hours had gone by before looking down at the glowing numbers on her watch and realizing that only twenty minutes had passed. She'll remember breaking into a stiff, aching sprint towards home, worried that her mother would be cross with her for being late.

Karen quietly closes the front door behind her and pauses in the hallway, listening to the blare of the television in the living room where Maria is doing her homework and the crackly hiss from the kitchen where her mother is cooking dinner. Upstairs, she locks herself in the bathroom, changes out of her uniform, and washes out the grass and mud stains with soap. She runs a hot flannel over her face, her arms, and her legs; no blood, no bruises. Why? Perhaps he heard people approaching and ran away before he had a chance to do anything. Perhaps he did some things, just not everything. Perhaps he only intended to scare her and panicked and fled when she passed out. Perhaps he had a change of heart. Whatever his intentions, Karen decides she cannot give him the chance again. She puts on her pyjamas and goes downstairs to the kitchen, where she announces her presence to her mother, apologizes for being late, and begins setting the table for dinner.

HONG KONG, 1941

"I've only a handful of years left," says Great Uncle Chutt.

"Great Uncle Chutt will live a long and fruitful life," replies Jun-Jun absently, dropping a piece of fish into his rice bowl.

"Like hell I will." The old man pushes his bowl away and pulls his pipe from his jacket pocket. "When I die, and it won't be long before I do, you'll have to manage all this on your own—the house, the farm, everything. Don't let things slide just because I'm not around."

"I'll do my best, Great Uncle Chutt."

Old man, thinks Jun-Jun, *when was the last time you picked up a broom or worked a plough?*

"I know you're capable enough. But this poor child…"

They both look at the idiot boy, picking through the fishbones on the table with his fingers.

"As his wife, it'll be your duty to make sure he doesn't go hungry."

LAST OF HER NAME

"His *wife?*"

"And don't let him leave the house without his clothes on. And keep him away from the chickens."

His mind is going, decides Jun-Jun. *Does he think we've already discussed this? No, Great Uncle Chutt doesn't discuss. Least of all with me.*

"And protect him from those thugs from Nam Po village."

Jun-Jun tells herself, *Just accept it until you find some other way.* She feels a knot in her chest and a tear forming in her left eye. She blinks it away.

"Yes, Great Uncle Chutt."

The old man claps his hands. "Good! Good!"

He lights his pipe, nodding as he sucks on the stem. "Destiny brought this boy into our home. I had no son, and then the Heavens gave me one." He pats the boy on the head. "First thing in the morning I'll tell the matchmaker to set an auspicious date. We'll keep the banquet small, just two or three tables. Mrs. Liu brought over oranges this afternoon—they're in a basket in the shed. Go and cut up a few for dessert."

"Orange!" The idiot boy licks his lips. "I want orange!"

"And pick the ripe ones with even coloring."

"Orange…" the idiot boy sings, beating time against the table with his fist, "Orange, orange, I want orange…"

"And leave the thin-skinned ones for last."

"…orange, orange…"

"Are you listening, Jun-Jun?!"

"Yes," says Jun-Jun. "Orange."

She pushes her chair from the table and marches out into the late, humid evening, across the concrete yard, towards the dim outline of the shed.

ENGLAND, 1973

June never lets her husband's hair crawl past his earlobes. She snips at it in the kitchen while Stanley closes his eyes against the swish of the scissor blades, the edges of his mouth pressed into a smile. After each new haircut he gets whistled compliments from the restaurant staff and soft, raised glances from Englishwomen. He sends his younger waiters to June when he thinks they're starting to look like hippies. They bring her gifts of fruit and refrain from coarse language, joking amongst themselves that she makes them all look like Chinese Steve McQueens. They don't articulate to each other what it is about the light, swift motion of her fingers in their hair that fills them with a strange longing—a combination of lust and homesickness—or the sobering effect of the cold, warning steel against their necks and ears.

June could still do this for a living if it weren't for the children. She is carrying their second child. They don't know yet that it's another girl, and are both openly wishing for a boy. *More troublesome*, says her husband, *but good for ensuring future generations of Leungs.*

June is the last of her name—Lam. Not that, as a female, she is responsible for preserving the name, and not that she'd ever got much use out of it. She's always just been "Jun-Jun." At home, or the farm, or later at the factory. When she'd worked on construction sites, men had called her other names, and she'd responded by pounding slabs of concrete into rubble at a faster pace, going home with a few more mun in her pocket. At the hair salon, the other hairdressers called her "Jun Je Je," Big Sister Jun. The waiters at the restaurant call her that, too, which somehow seems more respectful than the more formal "Mrs. Leung." Her

English neighbors call her "June," though it still takes her a moment to realize she's the one being addressed.

Names don't really matter, she thinks, as she snips away, releasing small tufts of her husband's hair to the floor. And although she'd be fine with having a boy, she secretly decides that namelines don't matter to her, either. What good is preservation, after all? Only survival matters.

ENGLAND, 1983

Karen spends her evenings and weekends re-watching episodes from her favorite mou hap videotapes: *The Return of the Condor Heroes*; *The Legend of the Condor Heroes* (a prequel), and *The New Heaven Sword and Dragon Sabre*. She also pores over the original novels that her father delightedly fetches for her from his bookshelf. She daydreams about being a noble warrior and flying over trees, blades flashing, transcending laws of gravity, utterly unburdened by daily oppressions. Her favourite mou hap heroes are those who come from humble origins and acquire mastery through diligent practice. She finds comfort in the reliable simplicity of their stories: they suffer tragedies, they meet their sifu (sometimes the first of many), and their journey of transformation begins.

Each night before bed, Karen goes to the window and peers behind the curtain down at the street. Ever since the attack, Ricky Stokes has taken up a nightly spot by the lamppost outside her house. He nurses one cigarette for as long as he can, and when he's finished with it, he stuffs his hands in his pockets and paces back and forth along the curb in an aimless fashion. Anyone would think he was waiting for a bus. Now and then his broad, bony face tilts up towards her window, his sunken eyes cast in shadow and his pale skin rendered a yellow-green hue by the tungsten glow of the lamp.

Karen tightens the handles on the windows before she gets into bed. Ricky Stokes could easily climb up the drainpipe to her room, but he hasn't, not yet. She tries to imagine another version of herself, a warrior self, one with the strength and daring to strike him down. She'd take the hammer from under her bed (her father hasn't noticed it missing from his toolbox) and knock him on his skull, or bludgeon his fingers to make him lose his grip and fall to his death. No, too much. Just paralyzed then.

One afternoon, June comes downstairs to find Karen doing push-ups in the living room.

"Doing exercise," says June, in a way that sounds more like a statement than a question. "School competition?"

Karen does five more push-ups and jumps to her feet.

"Just getting into shape," she says.

"That's good," says June.

June notices that ever since recovering from her fall, Karen seems to have acquired a sudden zeal for physical exertion. She rushes through her homework to run, skip, do push-ups and sit-ups. In the evenings, she ignores Maria's provocations, concentrating on her exercises, using weights she's fashioned from soda bottles filled with water.

One Saturday morning, June is washing dishes at the kitchen sink when she sees Karen kneeling on the back lawn and tying an empty oil canister to an old broom handle. June realizes she is trying to make a yoke-shaped set of dumbbells; this amuses her a moment, but only a moment. (Too soon she sees her child as a farmer, carrying water across burnt fields.) She walks out to the garden and taps Karen on the shoulder, who stiffens at her presence. The canisters are positioned too close to the center of the broom handle, and not tied securely enough. Karen moves aside so that June can kneel down next to her. She unties the ropes, then moves the canisters towards the ends of the broom handle and swiftly fastens them.

"It's stronger this way," she tells her daughter. "How did you get the idea?" A shrug. "Well, it's a good idea. Clever girl."

Karen tilts her head, shy from the praise. They remain a moment, kneeling side by side in front of the contraption. Finally, June gets up. She tells Karen to put a jacket on if she's going to stay outside. Then she heads towards the house, brushing imaginary blades of grass from her elbows and knees and contemplating the faint stretch of muscle along her daughter's shoulder.

For weeks, Karen has successfully avoided Ricky Stokes during the day. His attendance at school has become erratic, but she notices that when he does show up, his movements are still somewhat predictable. She sees him in the same places: lurking by the auditorium, smoking by the bike sheds, or looking bored and defiant on the bench outside the headmaster's office. Karen makes sure she's always in a group at lunch and between classes; no more reading by herself in the library, or on a bench in the schoolyard. Instead of walking home alone after school she joins the stream of students heading towards the town center to the bus stop or the burger restaurant. Karen breaks off at the roundabout by the church and ducks into The Golden Dragon, where her father has set aside a back table so she can do her homework, quietly pleased with her company. On busy evenings, she'll help clear and set tables, and at the end of the night, sometimes even before closing time, her father will drive them home, his favorite Cantonese ballads playing on the stereo. As they pull into their cul-de-sac, there's never any sign of Ricky Stokes waiting by the lamppost outside her house. But his absence doesn't give her any relief; she knows he'll turn up later.

On the night she decides to open the window, it's almost a full moon on a warm, cloudless evening. Ricky Stokes looks up in surprise and gives an awkward wave.

"Didn't think—" he quickly lowers his voice—"Didn't think you'd ever do that."

Karen shows him the hammer in her hand. "Go away. Stop coming here."

He raises his hands in surrender. "I just wanted to talk to you."

"Why?"

He lowers his head and starts nodding slowly, as if trying to recall lines he'd previously memorized. "What happened," he begins. "I didn't mean it. Cross my heart. It was meant to be a joke. Karen..."

To Karen's ears, there's something oddly pleading in the way he's talking to her, as if they're friends who've had a misunderstanding.

"Do you think you could forgive me one day? Karen?"

Karen hastily closes the window and puts the hammer back under the bed, then changes her mind and slips it under her blanket, holding it against her chest like a doll.

She recalls having once felt a little sorry for Ricky Stokes. All those stories that followed him around, though no one dared taunt him with them. She'd noticed that he still wore his summer uniform trousers in the winter, and that they hung above his ankles so he couldn't hide his grubby white socks. The torn collar on his shirt—it was always the same shirt— made her think of a dog whose ear had been bitten off in a fight. Perhaps he'd caught her staring at him once, had caught the sympathy in her eyes and been offended by it. Perhaps, she thought, this was his revenge.

HONG KONG, 1941

Idiot Boy is covered in shit. Jun-Jun prods his back with a stick and commands him to stand next to the bucket of water.

"This is what happens when you don't look where you're going," she hisses, ladling water over his head. He whimpers like a dog expecting to be kicked.

The crowd of villagers looks on from a safe distance, stifling giggles and waving their hands in front of their wrinkled noses. One of them, Brother Yuen, the fish seller, says he saw it all: the boy running along the stream, his arms outstretched and tongue hanging out, undeterred even when Brother Yuen began yelling at him for trampling his wife's lettuce heads.

"He just kept running and running, and—plop!—straight into the manure tank," Brother Yuen tells the crowd. "He screamed for help, but by the time I got there, Jun-Jun was already trying to pull him out with a rope. The whole time he was squealing like a pig being slaughtered! All that trouble, and for what, you might ask? Chasing a *dragonfly!*"

The villagers cannot help their snorting and cackling, though Brother Yuen is quick to add, "Little Sister Jun-Jun really is a saint, though. Strong, too."

Jun-Jun turns to the crowd, the edges of her mouth hardened somewhere between a grimace and a smile. "Forgive me for distracting you all from your very important business. Please don't waste another moment of your time on this worthless spectacle."

The villagers leave. Too slowly for Jun-Jun, but they leave. She regards her shit-covered husband-to-be. He's not whimpering anymore. Instead he's holding in his sobs with heaving, trembling effort.

"All right, all right," she soothes, ladling more water over his head, his shoulders, his legs. "Tell me, was it a nice dragonfly?"

He takes a few shuddering breaths before he's able to nod.

"Pink," he says, biting his lip. "It was pink."

ENGLAND, 1983

Occasionally Karen's mother will speak. While weeding the flowerbed or hanging out the laundry, she will quietly, casually throw out instructions—how Karen is holding herself wrong, how she needs to bend her knees a little here to stop from hurting herself. She tells her to breathe from the abdomen, not the upper chest; to be mindful of posture and correct alignment, how this will affect the direction of her chi. She'll briefly demonstrate a stance and say something like, "Strength is rooted in balance," then turn her back and retreat again into silent, domestic activity.

At first, Karen finds all of this an annoyance and ignores it. Eventually she tries one or two of her mother's suggestions, but only half-heartedly, expecting additional rejoinders. When the reproaches still do not come, she becomes curious. She starts to listen, trying to copy and string together the stances she's been shown, though it's hard to know whether she's doing anything correctly since her mother never comments on her progress; the most she'll do is repeat her instructions. Karen understands this as a sign of criticism, or then again perhaps a form of affirmation.

Gradually, she comes to see her mother differently. The familiar, comforting close-ups—fragments of a cheek, or a waist to wrap her arms around, or an arm to lean against—recede. What emerges in their place is a not entirely clear figure posing in a series of still lifes: a small, soft woman cutting vegetables or cooking dinner or washing up, hands hidden in dishes and soapy water. While Karen practices, her mother continues to give sparse, occasional instruction, but she's no longer alert to her mother's voice. She's paying attention instead to the evasiveness that meets her questions: How do you know all this? *There's not so much to know.* Did you have a sifu? A tribe? *Nothing like that.* Did you hurt anyone? *Silly girl. I used my hands to farm, to cut hair.*

The small, soft woman in the garden, by the stove, at the sink. Karen dares not call her a liar.

HONG KONG, 1941

Japanese planes tear through the sky. Villagers flee to the nearest shelters. Roofs shatter, windows explode. Fire, smoke, ravaged fields. Most are killed instantly. Eventually, the shelling stops. Survivors are rounded up and tortured, executed, raped. In minutes an entire village disappears. Almost.

ENGLAND, 1983

"Why aren't you asleep yet?" June is standing in the doorway.

"Don't hover by the window. You'll catch cold."

"You scared me," Karen grumbles, climbing into bed.

June straightens the curtains, then pulls the covers up around Karen's neck. Her voice is thick in the darkness. "Go to sleep." She smooths her daughter's forehead, brushing her fingertips across it like she did when the girls were little. "Close your eyes. Go to sleep. But in the morning we need to discuss the boy."

Earlier that night, June had startled the boy when she swung open the front door shouting, "Hey! What you doing there?"

After the boy had got a clear look at her—a diminutive, middle-aged Chinese woman—he'd straightened himself up and given a grim sort of laugh before walking away.

"Hey!" said June, opening the garden gate. "Come back here! Don't run away!"

June hadn't liked what she'd seen; the boy's casual lack of concern at being caught, his smirk as he turned to run. But most of all, she didn't like the fact that he'd been staring up at Karen's bedroom window with the oddest expression on his face: solemn and expectant, as if waiting for something inevitable to happen.

HONG KONG, 1941

Jun-Jun is squatting in a ditch behind the fields. The idiot boy is shaking and moaning, "My wrist! You're hurting meeeee...!" She puts her finger to her mouth to tell him *Quiet!* She mimes a salute to tell him *Soldiers!* (She knows the silence around them is a trick; she feels the soldiers' movements thudding through the earth, in the waters. They are close—fifty feet, maybe less.)

Still the boy struggles to his feet, dragging her up, "I'm... soooo... hung... greeee!" She twists his arm behind his back and clamps her other hand over his mouth. He wriggles and squirms, warm, moist sounds forcing their way through her fingers. She hisses into his ear, "Quiet! Do you want to die?!" She jabs him in the back of the thigh; he falls to his knees.

"Will you be good now?"

He nods, tears and snot running down his face. "I'll be good."

"Promise?" She softens her grip.

"Promise."

ENGLAND, 1983

After breakfast, June sits down opposite her daughter. Karen erupts into a tearful announcement. "I didn't do anything wrong. I didn't."

"Okay, okay," says June, patting her hand. "Just tell me what you know about the boy."

"What are you going to do?"

"That depends on what you tell me."

More than her mother's anger or concern, Karen dreads the prospect of having to hear herself describe things that she'd rather push out of her mind. But there is a calm, muted quality to her mother's questioning—"When was this?" "Then what happened?"—and a gentle, forward momentum that Karen finds reassuring, like being calmly pushed up a hill.

When Karen can't think of anything else to say, they sit in a silence that she mistakes at first for a kind of quiet consolation.

Then June says, "Do you know why he keeps coming back?

It's because he thinks there are no consequences. He's not afraid. So we must make him afraid." There is a stony resolve in her voice.

"Should we tell Father?"

June dismisses the notion with a curt shake of the head. "He would go too far without meaning to. And worse, he'd get caught. We'd lose everything, of course." She lifts her daughter's hands and squeezes them. "You keep practicing, yes? Grow your strength. The world is full of boys and men like Ricky Stokes, and you'll have to deal with them. But for now, let me take care of this one."

Karen nods, feeling she must acquiesce to the calm insistence in her mother's voice, the subtle grip of her hands.

"And we won't tell Father?" she asks.

"We won't tell anyone."

In the days and weeks that follow, Karen no longer sees Ricky Stokes outside her house at night. She doesn't see him at school or around town, and for several days she worries about what her mother might have done to him. She hears speculation around school that he's been sent away for some reason or other—house breaking or vandalism. Others say that his mother's latest boy-friend threw him out of the house after a violent argument, or that he got into trouble with a drug dealer and had to leave town. Every few months, someone will claim to have spotted him a few towns over, wiping tables in a pub or stacking shelves in a supermarket; such news will be met with rapidly diminishing concern. By the end of the school year, his absence will no longer be felt, and in due time, he will be all but forgotten by his teachers and peers.

HONG KONG, 1941

Eventually Jun-Jun and the idiot boy will climb out of the ditch and cross burnt fields. They will discover that everyone they know is dead.

Jun-Jun will take the boy with her into the city. One morning, she will lose him on a crowded street. In the days that follow, she'll hear that people are fleeing and manage to get on a boat to Macau. It will be years before she finds her way back to Hong Kong, many more before she boards a plane for England, and a few more again before she'll allow herself a moment now and then—eating dinner alone in a new country, or watching her daughters play-fighting in the garden—to think about how she lost the boy. If it had really been the force of a crowd, or if he'd panicked and struggled away from her grasp. Or perhaps she had been the one to struggle away, sensing an opportunity in the chaos. She'll never know what happened to him.

But for now, before any of that, the two of them huddle together in the ditch. And they wait.

THE WRONG DAVE

10-02-02
6:01 pm (GMT +7)

Okay, Dave. I forced myself to think about it all night and now, finally, I think I have an answer. I want you to know. Well, maybe I need a little more time. But I'm close...And when I've got it you'll be the first to know, okay? OK. // Yi

As the Thames reflects the grey morning sky, Dave Tang, a promising architect in his late twenties, stands in front of his drafting board full of ticks, looking to everyone else in the layered glass office as if he's thinking seriously about the new Nike store. He is not *not* thinking about the new Nike store, but he is thinking more about the email he received that morning from a drunk, interesting girl he met some years ago in Hong Kong. He doesn't, in fairness, know if she is still drunk, or even interesting, but since that is how she appeared to him the first and only time they met, and since she never acknowledged or responded to his efforts to keep in touch, and therefore forfeited opportunities to demonstrate other aspects of herself, he still only thinks of her as drunk and interesting.

He thinks about how to reply, imagining that he'll politely let her know of her mistake, that she is writing to the wrong Dave. Or he could just ignore it. He is mildly annoyed that after all this time—he calculates three years since they met at his cousin Pete's wedding—he is thinking about her again.

Dave wedges a finger under his shirt collar to relieve his neck, which has grown warm and a little damp. He looks at the email again. *I have an answer. I want you to know.* Yes, it's a mistake; she is writing to another Dave she knows. A Dave, he suddenly thinks, with whom she has bothered to keep in touch. He cannot help feeling a little peeved that the only time he hears from this girl in three years is by accident. In fact, he's surprised that he's peeved at all; it isn't that her lack of correspondence wounded him to the core and made him cynical about women or humanity or anything like that. He doesn't even recall having found her that attractive; she was bony and strange, her eyes too far apart. But something about her had appealed to him that night, and afterwards he'd been a bit hopeful, then disappointed when she hadn't written back.

He tells himself he shouldn't be so affected by this, and reminds himself of all the positive things in his life: his boss acknowledges his talent and expresses confidence in him, and he'll be marrying Mayling in the spring—beautiful, accomplished Mayling, who works for an important U.S. law firm and doesn't mind his cheerful ignorance about subjects that inspire in her a diligent curiosity, such as nature, the arts, and European history. Also, the builders finally completed work on the kitchen last weekend, all open-plan cinderblock and brushed chrome. He shouldn't be affected by this email. But it is a painful reminder that he once offered himself to this girl and his efforts had not even merited a rejection; he had simply been ignored. And he can't help but allow himself to wonder, just a little, what it is that she has spent all night thinking about.

An hour later:

10-02-02
7:00 pm (GMT +7)

Do you believe in an afterlife, Dave? I'm asking because it could have something to do with what happened yesterday. I should back up. A couple of weeks ago, my blind grandma told me she could see again. At first I thought, oh my God it's a miracle! But no. She saw things that weren't there—warriors on horses, fire-breathing dragons, tiny children in white hats. My whole life, I never heard her say anything that sounded even a little bit crazy. But she was dead serious, so I played along. I asked, "Where are they, Popo?" and she pointed to the foot of the bed. She explained that she wasn't scared, but they were exhausting her because they wouldn't leave her alone. She said she hadn't slept for days. Then she started swatting the air in front of her, trying to make the hallucinations go away. I didn't know what to do so I just joined in. I started swinging at the air shouting, "Get! Go! Fuck off, dragon! Fuck off, tiny children!" but when I stopped Popo said, "No, keep going, they're still there." So I kept going until my voice and arms were sore. But after all that effort she told me they were still there.

At first she wondered if she was hallucinating because of the cataract surgery or the new medication. Then she wondered if she had dementia. But Popo's daughters—my Aunt Flora and Aunt Mei—had another theory. They told me that people who are close to death, usually the old and the sick, they start experiencing hallucinations that are actually glimpses of the afterlife. I don't know if that's a Chinese thing or just their thing, but they believed it enough to tell Popo that her visions of warriors, dragons, and little kids were there to lead her towards the light. Maybe Popo believed that, too, and she was following the visions when she jumped. Or maybe she killed herself because she just wanted her suffering to end.

The police said she must have jumped from the living room window, as it was the only window in the apartment that would've given her a clear fall, no obstructions, for twelve floors. She would've had to wait for a wash day, the only time her helper Suli would unlock the window grille to hang out the laundry. After a week of rain, the sun finally came out yesterday. Popo would have waited until Suli finished the laundry and left for the market. Then Popo must have felt her way to the living room, climbed onto the ledge, pushed a wet shirt out of the way, and jumped.

I thought about this all night, and this is the closest I've come to getting my head around what happened, what was going through her mind. Maybe it wasn't like this, all calm and methodical. Maybe it was done in a burst of panic or inspiration. I'm really just trying to understand. These are only thoughts. Oh, I forgot to ask you last time—how are things with you? // Yi

Now Dave is not only peeved but also somewhat depressed. He doesn't want to think about a suicide during his work day. Then he feels like a bad sort of person. Mayling sometimes calls him insensitive, which most of the time he considers unfair and perplexing. Now that he's learned about the suicide, he feels involved, even though his involvement is a mistake. Can he uninvolve himself? No, no, he must stop. He has deadlines. He'll do the right thing and come clean. In his reply, he'll express sympathy for her loss, but also say that he believes she has the wrong Dave, which is quite all right, could happen to anyone, blah blah blah. He might add that it was still nice to hear from her, and you know, no hard feelings about not having kept in touch over the years, happens to the best of us, and that he wishes her all the best. No, no, too petty and insincere, and he sounds too ho ho British. He'll have to work on this a bit. Maybe at lunch. For now, he needs to turn his attention to the Nike store.

The rest of his day:

1:00 pm. Instead of staying in the office to write his reply, Dave goes out for pizza with his colleagues Nathan and Tony. They go to a new place on the other side of the river called Angelo's. Dave orders extra anchovies by mistake.

2:15–4:00 pm. Dave is distracted by thoughts of Yi; he does not make the progress he had hoped to.

4:05–4:56 pm. Furthermore, he does not pay full attention during the project meeting; at one point the Netherlands Nike representative catches him staring out the window with his mouth open.

6:01 pm. He calls Mayling and tells her he'll have to stay late.

7:25 pm. Mayling calls and asks how much later he'll be, and Dave says he doesn't know, catching the sharpness in his voice. She says she just got home and was going to order food and wanted to know if she should wait for him to eat. He says sorry and tells her if she could save some leftovers that would be nice.

8:45 pm. Dave comes home. His neck hurts. He kisses Mayling, who is watching TV on the sofa with her arms around her knees. She kisses him back, but in a distracted sort of way. She is concentrating on a documentary about the Roman Colosseum. Dave makes a comment about the kitchen looking good. Mayling mumbles agreement to the TV. Dave takes his dinner out of the large titanium fridge: black bean ribs, his favourite. But he's too tired to think about how to work the new stove or the microwave or hunt for utensils. He could ask Mayling, but she'd just shout instructions, and he'd say *What? Where?* She would then have to get up, leaving the Roman Colosseum, and, going to the kitchen, heat up his dinner and find him utensils with a faster than usual efficiency that would make him feel nervous and guilty. So instead, Dave sits at the cinderblock island and eats the ribs cold with his hands.

Later, when Mayling is asleep:

10-02-02
11:30 pm (GMT)

Dear Yi,
Sorry about your grandmother. That's really shit.

(Delete)

10-02-02
11:30 pm (GMT)

Dear Yi,
So sorry about your grandmother. I'm glad you feel you can talk to me about it.

(Too touchy feely. Also a bit creepy. Delete)

10-02-02
11:31 pm (GMT)

Hello!
Do you even know who you're writing to?

(Do I have to be such a wanker? Delete)

10-02-02
11:31 pm (GMT)

Dearest Yi,
I had a shit day at work today and it's all because of your
fucking morbid email.

(Delete)

10-02-02
11:32 pm (GMT)

Yi,
I'm fine, thanks. Sorry to hear about your Popo. How are
you doing? Tell me more if you want. Dave

(Send)

* * *

Dave's cousin Pete and Pete's fiancée Pauline must have spent many fraught evenings rehearsing their thank you speech, which they eventually delivered in the summer of 1999 to their five hundred and thirty-two guests in the ballroom of the Hong Kong Marriott Hotel. After the applause, a young woman in a pink Rolling Stones t-shirt stood up in the middle of the room and thrust her champagne glass in the direction of the stage, causing nearby guests to duck for cover. With much feeling, she proclaimed her admiration for the couple in slurry Cantonese. "You are such a beautiful example of mutual love and respect. How you—sorry, I didn't catch your name, sir—"

"Uh, Pete," said Pete.

"How you, Pete, look at her like she's your queen. And *you*, Mrs. Pete, you look at him like he's a fucking gladiator...You guys should finish your champagne, get the hell out of here, and fuck each other's fucking brains out..." She drained the glass and held it above her head like a trophy.

One of the guests—a tall, unsmiling man in a blazer—stood up, pried the glass out of her hand, and took her by the shoulders. The other guests stared and clutched their napkins as he turned her towards the double doors and walked her out, still talking about love and admiration. She seemed happy enough to be walked. The doors closed behind them, leaving the room in uncomfortable silence. Then Pete cleared his throat and made a joke about alcoholics, and everyone laughed. Dave, who was sitting at the next table, felt a little bad for the girl.

At the end of the evening, after the newlyweds had retired to their room and the last of the guests had trickled out into the night, Dave happened upon the Rolling Stones girl in the lobby. She was slumped in a fat armchair in front of the slow trickling fountain full of chubby, bronze cupids. He tapped her on the arm.

"Miss, are you okay?" he asked in Cantonese. She nestled her cheek into the back of her chair in a drowsy-eyed, childish sort of way. Dave took the chair facing her and tried again in English.

"Are you okay? Can I get a taxi for you?" When she still didn't answer, he added, "Nice speech. I mean it."

She looked up at him with a grimace. "I've never done this before," she said. "Crashing a wedding. Crashing anything."

Dave said he believed her, and that it was all right. She shook her head. No, no, she wanted to explain. She was a camera operator for TVB and had spent all day shooting a drama about three feuding generations of oil tycoons.

"The director's a moron," she said, "and after being yelled at all day I just wanted to be somewhere else before going home to bed. I was going to meet a friend at the hotel bar, but he stood me up, and I ended up drinking by myself. The bartender asked me if I was escaping the wedding, and I said what wedding, and—well, you know the rest."

Dave noticed that she spoke English comfortably, though her American accent was cut with a grating, local staccato that hurt his ears a little. She said that at first she'd been having a great time at the banquet, but now she felt horrible for ruining what was meant to be a special occasion, and for eating other people's food. Dave patted her hand and assured her it was fine. They sat in silence for a while. Then he told her a joke, which made her smile. She said she knew some jokes, too, and told him five in succession, each one a variation on why the chicken crossed the road. Dave found none of them funny, but still he smiled, not out of politeness, but at the fact that she found them so hysterical; at one point she actually slapped her thigh. When she laughed, he noticed her wide, uneven teeth. Her eyes were large and far apart, and she barely blinked. This put him a little on edge, though he tried to ignore this. He told her the earring in her left ear, a tangle of blue-green beads and feathers, looked like a fishing lure. She said, "Thanks, I made it myself." He wanted to touch it, but thought perhaps he shouldn't. She told him his suit made him look too serious and much too old. She was smiling at him. Or rather, her eyes were smiling, while her mouth was twisted into what very much resembled a frown. She would not look away. Dave's neck was growing hot and damp under her gaze. He felt they were trapped in this moment, in the warm, heavy stillness between her curious smile-frown and his damp neck.

His damp neck.

Dave hadn't meant to speak, hadn't even realized his mouth had started to move, but he found himself blurting out the name of his hotel and their proximity to it.

She looked a little confused. Then thoughtful. Then she turned her gaze to the bronze cupids in the fountain and proceeded to stare at them for a long time. Dave was wondering when his mouth had started operating independently from his brain, and, more importantly, why. Finally, she turned back to him.

"That's a nice hotel," she said. "My friend Donny works there. He can get you a discount—just ask for him when you check out. Donny Chow. Got that? Tell him Yi said hi."

Dave thanked her. She said it wasn't a problem. Then there seemed to be nothing else to say. They shook hands, exchanged business cards, and said they'd keep in touch.

On the flight back to England the next morning, Dave thought mostly about the projects that were waiting for him when he got back. He felt unenthusiastic about two (a commission for a Buddhist visitor centre in Hertfordshire and a radio tower in Warwickshire), and vaguely excited about one (a corporate flight centre in Michigan). He thought about his girlfriend Mayling, and how, though they'd argued before he left, he was looking forward to seeing her. Even though they'd only been seeing each other for a few months, he had already become used to her and her ways: how she automatically leaned in to show her attentiveness when someone talked to her; her skeptical way of saying, "Are you sure?" when he corrected her on the British version of a word (she was still unconvinced by *aluminium*); her trepidation towards large dogs; her small ears, always cold; and more recently, now that she'd started staying over, how she got hungry in the middle of the night, slipping out of bed slowly and carefully to avoid waking him, though she always did and he never told her.

He also thought about the drunk, interesting girl from the night before. Yi. He regretted having mentioned his hotel, and at the same time wondered why he hadn't tried a little harder to get her to go back with him.

The following week he thought about her sporadically, each time very briefly, and with a different question: What was she thinking as she stared at the chubby cupids in the fountain? Had she been at all tempted to go back with him? Was she having some kind of moral struggle? If she had gone back with him, would the sex have been any good? (Dave wavered between three scenarios: wild and animalistic / tender and full of meaning / awkward and polite, both regretting it as they were doing it.)

Or would they have had sex at all? Perhaps they would have talked all night, or perhaps she would have passed out and he would have watched TV. Well, he doubted he'd ever see her again. They didn't seem to have much in common, and he wasn't sure that he even found her that attractive. But he was somehow also strangely reluctant to let her float away so easily. And he felt, for reasons unclear to himself, that it was important that she didn't think of him as a moron. He decided to write to her. He kept the email brief and friendly. In it, he said how nice it was to have met her and that he hoped things were going well for her. He wrote something that made reference to one of the jokes she'd told that night, hoping it would create a tone of familiarity and that she'd appreciate that he was a person who paid attention.

When a week passed and she hadn't replied, he wrote a second email, but because he didn't want to appear too pushy or desperate, he decided instead to re-send the first email, prefaced with a lie about problems with his account and people not receiving emails and him having to re-send the as a result. After a week and a half, he sent the second email. When she still hadn't replied two weeks after that, he wondered if she'd found him too presumptuous, or simply too straight-laced. She probably liked musicians. Then he decided that the most likely explanation was that she'd been too drunk to remember him. He let it go, never hoping or expecting that she might think of him again—much less that three years later, when he was about to marry Mayling, she would finally reach out to him.

The day after sending his reply to Yi, Dave checks his inbox twice before lunch and three more times over the rest of the afternoon. She has not replied. Dave wonders if she's realized her mistake in emailing the wrong Dave. Then he wonders if she's done something to harm herself, though the probability of this seems small to him. He has an idea that she has more to say, and that until she's said it, she isn't likely to be going anywhere. He wants to know what happens next. He wants to know whether she will acknowledge the sensitivity of his reply. *How are you doing? Tell me more if you want.* He reads his email to her twice, thinking to himself, yes, he definitely has his moments.

A little after five o'clock he joins his colleagues for happy hour at a nearby pub. Dave nurses one ale as Nathan and Tony finish one round, then another, then start on tequila shots. Dave envies their ability to sustain their bubble of loud, happy inebriation, and suddenly resents Nathan, his best friend and soon-to-be best man, for having given up on Dave's "booze-training" back in college. A second beer or glass of wine is enough to take him down—he'll feel uncomfortably warm, then nauseous, then likely throw up before passing out. He knows himself and his limits. But as the stars start appearing in the polluted night sky, his desire to get drunk grows stronger and stronger. Finally, he downs one, two, three tequila shots. Ten minutes later, he passes out.

10-03-02
4:05 pm (GMT +7)

Popo's son identified the body. It was the first time I'd seen Uncle Yun cry. When he started describing her face, he said there wasn't anything left that looked like her. I can't believe she did it like that. She could have taken pills, I would've helped her if she wanted. But she made it so public. Did she think about how it would make us feel, how it would look? I can hear the rumors now, about the old lady in 12C who went blind and then her kids abandoned her and then she went crazy as well and threw herself out the window. That's what people are like here, Dave, especially the old vultures in the building who called themselves her friends. Popo let herself become another piece of gossip, and part of me wonders if that was part of her plan: to publicly shame us—me, Uncle Yun, Aunt Mei, and Aunt Flora—for neglecting her.

I made the mistake of going straight back to work today. The crew was in Mongkok this morning, stuck in traffic, and Yung the sound guy was bitching on his phone to someone—"Yeah the intersection's completely blocked, some guy on the roof of the 7-11's been threatening to jump for like thirty minutes and the cops are trying to get him down. Man, if you're gonna jump, hurry up and do it already! Some of us have places to go!" I mean, I know this attitude is pretty common here—people complain about jumpers all the time—but God, when he said that I just wanted to punch him. Instead I start sweating and crying and looking like a freak. Yeah, suddenly I'm one of those sensitive assholes with no sense of humour. But I'm kind of new to all this. I mean, my mother died, but I was a baby at the time so I don't remember her at all. Popo was the one who raised me. She was my mother. Now she's gone. The only thing I can be sure of is that everything's going to feel different. I'm sorry, Dave. You've caught me in a shitty mood. I'll be better next time. I'm glad one of us is fine. It's just that I have to expel some of this feeling, and somehow I know you'll help me send some of this away. But don't just let me go on and on with my sad shit. Tell me what's new. How's your life, your work, your girl, etc etc // Yi

Dave, hungover and regretful at his desk, wonders what he would have done about Yung the sound guy. When was the last time he hit someone? He thinks it might have been in Edinburgh, after a football match while he was still at university. Yes, he remembers now, late afternoon, low light, walking down Princes Street with Nathan and being ambushed by a group of football fans—there were four of them, he recalls, jumping on them from behind. He remembers *Chink!*, boots and fists, blood, the slow passing feet of onlookers. He remembers brief, muddled euphoria, then embarrassment. Nathan had his right arm broken; Dave lost two front teeth. He borrowed money from friends so he could get his teeth replaced without his parents finding out. It surprises him that he hasn't thought about it again until now.

He thinks about Yung the sound guy and believes that yes, he would have hit him. Yi sounds so grateful. He is actually helping. But now she's asking for information. *How's your girl?* That could mean girlfriend or wife or daughter. Dog? He decides to play it safe and keep to generalities:

10-03-02
9:25 am (GMT)

Yi,
You kept your cool, that's good. I would've hit the wanker.

Not much news at this end, same old, same old. Work good. Girl good. Just got a new kitchen installed. Girl excited about it. How are you now? Take your time, okay? Dave

He doesn't hear from her for the rest of the day, or the day after, and he worries that she's onto him. Maybe she's writing to an American Dave, and he gave away his Britishness. Maybe he shouldn't have said "wanker." And perhaps American Dave wouldn't have installed a kitchen. Perhaps American Dave is a hippy and lives in a yurt. Perhaps he's Native American, a wise Dave who dispenses much better advice than *Take your time, okay?*

That evening over dinner, Dave and Mayling have a disagreement about the wedding invitations. The village hall, she says, can now only manage sixty people, not eighty, something about new fire regulations. When Dave says, *All right then, let's see who we can take off the list,* Mayling is quick to point out that at least fifteen people on his side are extraneous. *You haven't spoken to some of these people in years,* she says. *What about your side?* he says. She is reluctant. *These people are all important.* He can't understand why she has so many bloody friends. *You don't even like some of them,* he says. *You called that Steve Whatshisname a two-faced snake who's been after your job since day one, remember?* Mayling says he is not being helpful. Dave says she has double standards. Mayling calls him selfish. He calls her difficult and hypocritical. They continue in this manner for several days.

10-08-02
2:17 pm (GMT +7)

What does your new kitchen look like? It sounds so cool.
I know I haven't written for a few days. Funeral arrangements. My uncle and aunts want to take the traditional
Chinese route, even though it's a total circus the way the
children are meant to parade their atonement for their
parent's sins, pray for the safe passage of the soul to the
other side, etc, etc. Popo doesn't need her sins atoned for.
She didn't do anything wrong.

I have this friend from the States who's like, oooh,
Eastern religion, and gets all awestruck when we see a
monk on the street or riding the MTR. I tell him, you
Westerners don't know shit. Monks are as bad as Catholic
priests, and they steal too.

But my uncle and aunts want to be shoved around by
a bunch of jerks in yellow robes and told when to kneel,
when to pray, where to sit, what to burn…twenty-three
hours of this! It will be torture, and they will love it and
need it, a sado-masochistic fake catharsis.

I know I have no seniority in this family, no authority to
speak on important matters. But I remind them that Popo
got baptized in her seventies by missionaries who came to
the village, so technically she was a Christian. And because
Popo was the kind of person who liked to have things done
right, I'm sure she would have wanted a Christian service.
Why do I say all this? I don't know, but I'm absolutely prepared for a fight. Check it out—in this corner, me, defender
of the Christian faith, haha! In the other corner, Uncle Yun,

the Taoist. In another corner, Aunts Mei and Flora, the ritu-al-heavy Buddhists, all superstitions and flipfloppy beliefs. I am so prepared for a fight. I tell them that it's not about religion, it's about honoring her wishes for once. And you know what, Dave? They actually give in. Funeral's next week. It will be awful. Oh well. // Yi

Dave wonders if he should suggest seeing a doctor or thera-pist, then thinks better of it. Yi might take offense. She might stop writing. Dave feels highly unqualified. He wonders if he is still helping. He thinks it's a good sign that she asked about the kitchen. At least she shows interest in other things besides death and anger. He senses that she's not very religious. Perhaps she doesn't even believe in God. Dave and Mayling are planning a church wedding, though he hasn't attended a service in years. Sundays have long been reserved for five-a-side games with the Latymer Old Boys Football Club, and more recently, on May-ling's insistence, post-game dimsum with his parents. (In May-ling's presence, his parents transform into animated, interested human beings with questions and opinions on a variety of topics. Dave finds this somewhat unnatural and disturbing. Whenever Mayling leaves the table, a familiar quiet falls upon the Tangs; the three of them stare into the middle distance, or at the food.)

Dave doesn't think a person has to attend church regularly to be a good Christian. But he can't recall the last time he prayed, or even thought deeply about God. He believes he is far from the model Christian, but also that he's surely a little better than those who don't believe in anything. How can a person not believe in anything? He considers asking Yi this question.

10-09-02
3:03 pm (GMT)

Dear Yi,
I've attached a photo of the kitchen. As you can see it's pretty cool and modern looking, very clean lines. Cinderblock, brushed chrome, and rosewood. Haven't used it as much as I'd like. Usually back late from work and too knackered. So is girl.

Hope the funeral goes OK. Re: Christian services—I'd say it really depends on the priest. Some are boring and go on. Others are pretty decent. Some even tell jokes.

Anyway, the main thing is that you're doing what your grandmother wanted, and that's really good. I'm sure your uncle and aunts are going through a difficult time, too.

Take care,
Dave

10-11-02
3:56 pm (GMT +7)

Maybe you're right, Dave. Maybe I'm being too hard on them. I've been so hung up on how they treated Popo that I forget how nice it used to be. Growing up, it was mostly just me and Popo doing our thing in the village, but my uncle and aunts would come back every Sunday for hot pot or barbecue. Summers I went into the city to hang out at my Uncle Yun's electronics store in Sham Shui Po. He let me pull apart cameras and amplifiers and shit, which is probably why I became such a gadget junkie. Aunt Flora would swing by and take me to the mall for ice-cream or a movie. Aunt Mei would cut out articles for me about medicinal roots and herbs. Popo knew all about that stuff, too, but she couldn't read. This, for them, was love. But they never talked about real stuff, never talked to me about my mother. Popo would. She said I was sweet like her, and that I had her big eyes, her curiosity, and her bad teeth, haha. She told me about the bus crash and how nine other people were killed, one of them a baby. She didn't say much about my dad, just that he was some city boy who didn't hang around too much longer after my mother died.

So back then, things were pretty good. What changed? I finished high school and decided I needed to explore the world. So for a couple of years I worked my butt off and saved like crazy. I worked in my uncle's store, in a warehouse, at McDonald's, I was even one of those beer promotion girls for a while. The day I left for the States, Popo said she was so proud of me. She didn't care that I was going to a crummy community college in a crummy beach town. To her, someone who never got the chance to go to school, I was flying to the Gold Mountain to get an Important American Education. I took film classes, learned to pronounce Truffaut, and got into surfing and pot. In the meantime, Popo's house got too much for her to manage on her own. She got cataracts, then glaucoma. She let my uncle sell the house and move her into a nursing home closer to town. She didn't last a month there—she was lonely and depressed because the other residents never spoke to her and the nurses were bullies. So my uncle and aunts found her a small apartment in Tsuen Wan and hired a live-in helper from Indonesia called Suli. The first day, they showed Suli where everything was. The second day they went back to check on her. Then it was another week before they went back. Then another two, three weeks would go by before any of them would visit. When I phoned from the States, Popo always said she was fine, that her kids were over there all the time. It was only when I came back to Hong Kong and visited her in that dark, pokey apartment that Suli took me aside and told me everything. "Popo sad," she said. She was learning Cantonese. "Popo lonely. Nobody come."

I read this book once about this teenage boy who stabs an old woman in the eyes with model aeroplanes and leaves them in the sockets. Actually I never finished it because I had to stop after that. I mean, what kind of sick fucker would write a story like that? Are all families this disappointing? // Yi

The next day, Dave and Mayling meet his parents for dimsum and negotiations over the invitation list for the Hong Kong reception, which Dave doesn't really want. In fact, he doesn't really want the English village hall reception either. With the newly slimmed down invitation list, Mayling has decided that the original seating arrangements are no good and must be changed. Dave secretly wonders why they can't simply take away a few chairs here and there. Nevertheless, the two of them have plans to take the train up to the Lake District that weekend so they can pace the village hall and take measurements and photos.

If it were up to him, he'd have the two of them elope. He's heard about people who run off to Las Vegas to get married with five-dollar rings by a minister who looks like Elvis. He thinks this would be fun. Tie the knot, hit the casino, catch a show—this doesn't sound too bad at all. Or Nathan could get ordained over the Internet and marry them on a beach in the Maldives. They'd honeymoon there, take surfing lessons. Yi surfs. As his parents and Mayling pick through the list of cousins, aunts, and uncles (once, twice, three times removed) from the UK, America, and Hong Kong, then former school friends, colleagues, and employers, Dave stares at the shrimp dumplings growing cold and sweaty in the steam basket and wonders if Mayling could ever be persuaded.

As soon as Dave and Mayling return to the flat, Dave hurries to the study and pulls up in front of the computer. He can't tell if he's trembling from the cold or from excitement.

10-14-02
9:03pm GMT

Yi,
I've just come back from the Lake District. I'm supposed to be getting married there in a few months. I should have mentioned this before. The truth is, I don't know if—

"Where are you?" Mayling is calling from the living room or the kitchen.

"In the study!" Dave shouts. The panic in his voice surprises him.

"You just threw your bags on the floor!"

Dave makes an effort to sound normal. "Can you put the kettle on? I'll be out in a minute!"

> The truth is, I don't know if this is what I want.
> I need to think. I should go away for a while. I have my ticket for Hong Kong. We're having a reception there as well. Fuck. I have to talk to Mayling. That's my fiancée. She'll be—

Dave looks at what he's just written. He deletes it all and starts again:

> I need to see you. I need—

He reads the line once, twice, three times. He notices that his neck is warm and damp. So are his palms. A message arrives:

> 10-14-02
> 4:06 am (GMT +7)
>
> Hi Dave. We had the funeral today at a memorial hall

in Tai Wai. The Christian service successfully alienated everyone present. I watched my uncle and aunts squirm at each mention of Jesus and stare dumbly at their English hymn books and throw dagger eyes at me. But it's okay. It's all token anyway. Uncle Yun is having a Taoist ceremony in a couple of days. They'll find her a nice altar place in the temple. I always knew this was going to happen. I just wanted them to do one last thing for Popo, the way she would have wanted it. And to suffer a little more. If only you were here. We could go sit on the beach and share this bottle of bad whisky. I don't feel good. // Yi

Dave is thrilled—for the first time he and Yi are online at the same time. He imagines her in her beach shack, sand between her toes, her face illuminated by the glow of the computer screen. He notices the time on the email. She's drinking. She's clearly distraught. She needs him there. It won't feel like an imposition. He looks back over his line and makes some changes:

If you want, I can come and see you—

He can change the date on his ticket and fly to Hong Kong in a matter of days—but the problem is that he's used up all his holiday time for the wedding. Though thinking about it more, he still has sick leave that he hasn't yet taken, and he could even possibly use some of the holiday time originally intended for the wedding. He just has to talk to Mayling.

If you want, I can come and see you—

He is sweating enough that he can smell himself: damp, sour heat. He licks his palm. Salty. He can hear Mayling moving things around in the kitchen; the clink of a teaspoon, the opening and shutting of cupboards. It all sounds familiar and somehow pitiful. All he needs to do is get up, go to her, speak: *I'm sorry, I can't get married.*

10-14-02
4:10 am (GMT +7)

So Dave, I have a question for you. What happens when you die? Uh-oh, time's up! Read the following information very, very carefully…

After the funeral we took the shuttle to the train station. There was a stall by the entrance selling cheap sunglasses and Hello Kitty toys, techno music blasting out of one of those flimsy stereos from Shenzhen (techno— can the idiotic be evil???), while the vendors, two young women, all nails and highlights, pored over the Apple Daily and talked about some movie star's affair. Want to know what happens when you die? THIS. This is what happens—Hello Kitty, crappy sunglasses, blue chips, red chips, fish and chips, pollution, fucking bad, bad music. The rest of the world goes on. LIFE GOES ON, blah blah blah. As it should. It's obscene that it should. Us being here is obscene.

Are you there? // Yi

Dave looks over his line—*If you want, I can come and see you*— and decides it is inadequate.

10-12-02
9:15 pm (GMT)

Yi,
Yes, I'm here! Sorry you're going through all this. I wish I could be there. In fact, I have a ticket—

"Dave! We're out of PG Tips!"
"What?"
"We're out of PG Tips!"
"Well, then, don't worry about it!"
"But the water's boiled! Don't you want something else?"
"Okay!"

I have a ticket, and I can come to you. I can—

"Like what? Coffee? Chamomile? Look, I'm sick of yelling..."
Dave hears Mayling's footsteps approaching and he hastily

goes to meet her in the hallway. He is surprised by what he sees. She looks smaller, pale. She still has her beige raincoat on, and her hair is frizzed about her face from the damp. Her lips are pale and slightly cracked, and her eyeliner has smudged beneath the outer corners of her eyes. He notices that she's holding a white teacup in her hand. He has never seen her look so slovenly or bewildered; he suddenly feels overcome with affection.

"Are you all right?" he asks, lightly stroking her cheek.

"A bit tired," she replies.

"Let me make the tea."

"No, it's fine," she says.

"Let me," he insists, attempting to coax the cup from her grasp. She slaps him away.

"Ow," says Dave, rubbing his hands.

"Sorry," she says. "I was worried you'd break it. Now, come with me and tell me what you want."

He follows her to the kitchen, where she starts pulling out boxes of herbal teas from the cupboard and lining them up on the cinderblock island.

"I really wanted some PG Tips. But it looks like we're out," she says, picking through the boxes.

Dave notices that she has put the teacup on the counter. He wonders if now is a good time to tell her. He imagines her throwing the teacup at him, her face red with anger. She'd throw it at him, and he'd duck, and it would smash against the wall. Standing among the little shards, she'd fire questions, *Why, When, How?* Or she wouldn't throw the teacup at him; she'd put it down on the counter and look for something unbreakable to lob at him to minimize damage and mess—the plastic orange salad bowl, for example, the one he bought from IKEA that she was embarrassed to use when they had his parents over for dinner. The salad bowl would bop him on the head and land on the floor, spinning; she'd pick it up and continue hitting him on the head with it while firing questions, *Why, When, How?* The thought makes him smile a little. Or perhaps she'd surprise him and not throw anything or ask questions. Perhaps she'd just stand there blankly, holding her teacup. Maybe she'd get very quiet, very calm, and after a moment announce that she has to leave. Or she'd ask *him*, quietly and calmly, to leave. Which he would. He'd pack a bag, call Nathan. This third scenario feels like the worst one, the saddest. It occurs to Dave then, as Mayling holds up a sachet of peppermint tea and he nods and she drops it into the teacup and fills it with hot water, that it doesn't take much to change everything: get up, go to her, speak. It doesn't take much to cause deep, irreversible pain. The prospect is terrifying and thrilling.

"Let it steep for a couple of minutes," says Mayling, handing him the teacup.

He tells her to leave it on the counter.

"I'll come back out for it. I've just got to finish this email."

Dave returns to the study, closes the door behind him and sits down. He continues:

> I have a ticket, and I can come to you. But I need to sort things out here. I have to explain to Mayling

He stops. There are two new messages in his inbox:

10-14-02
4:16 am (GMT +7)

Let me tell you this: I am sick. I am disgusting and wrong. I am sick of sadness, anger, guilt. It's become such a part of me that I can't remember how my body feels without it. A badge, a license. No, no. That's tragic. I won't be one of those. I am one of those.

I tried, I did. To make you happy, give you some good moments. Convince you that you were loved, you really were. I let you bitch about your children and afterwards tried to make excuses for them. Where did they all go? You got so tired, and so did I. The same picture, you sitting on your bed, eyes open, expecting, waiting for something I don't know what. For me? Popo, I'll take you outside, go on feel the sunshine. Don't wait for me, I've run out of ideas, I don't know what to do.

10-14-02
4:25 am (GMT +7)

It's so nice when it finally stops raining. Today is blazing hot, glorious sun. Suli slides the wet garments out onto the metal poles. She smiles at the fortress of identical high rises because it looks like a holiday out there, a new, non-religious, urban festival. But instead of flags and streamers there are shirts, towels, pillowcases, pants, socks, bras, bedsheets, all waving brightly in celebration of the weather. She thinks of Indonesia. She misses her family. Her work done, she says Bye! I'm leaving for market now! and Popo says Bye! Don't forget to pay the electric bill! Popo sits upright in her bed like a good child, eyes open, waiting for the slam of the iron gate and the elevator ding and its grinding downwards. Then slowly she pulls herself up, sits on the edge of the bed. She wiggles her feet into her hard plastic slippers.

She gets up and begins slow, careful steps, arms out, moving through the small, glowing children...through the warriors and their angry, rearing horses...through the dragonfire. There's the door frame, the wall. There's the hard edge of the dining table. There's the windowsill. She climbs onto the ledge, pushes a damp shirt out of the way. Maybe she's thinking, this will be over soon, and she's glad that she'll finally have some peace. Or, this is a terrible mistake, what have I done, forgive me. Or is she thinking only of the cold on her skin, or of the children playing below in the courtyard who will have to see her shattered corpse on the ground, or is she unable to think of anything at all because the shock has already killed her before she hits the ground?

Dave turns the computer off and sits in front of the blank, crackling screen.

"Are you done?" Mayling comes in and puts the teacup on the desk.

"Oh, I'd forgotten about that," says Dave.

"I know," she says, resting her chin on his head. "Was it important?"

"What?"

"The email you were writing."

She hangs her arms over his shoulders; he takes her hands, squeezing them.

"You're cold," he says.

"Tired."

"Let's leave the unpacking till tomorrow. I'll get a bath going."

Mayling nods. "Sounds good."

Over the following months, preparations for the wedding take shape: guest lists are finalized; invitations sent out; speeches written, edited, rehearsed. Dave wants everything to go smoothly and decides that the easiest way to achieve this is to go along with everything Mayling wants.

He does not hear from Yi. He assumes that, for whatever reason, he is no longer needed. He discovers that he doesn't mind this, and instead of resentment or indignation, it is guilt that he feels.

He still hasn't replied to her last correspondence; what could he possibly say? He feels he ought to at least acknowledge her situation. But no, he would never be able to leave it at that. He'd want to say more and not be able to. He can't offer comfort or advice. He doesn't want to tell her about himself, that he has been having dreams, nightmares really, in which it's dark all the time, he can't see, can barely hear anything except the sound of aeroplanes. He doesn't want to tell her that he feels indecent, wrong and unqualified for knowing all that he has come to know about her, that sometimes when Mayling is out or asleep he reads her emails and afterwards feels craven and sickened and wonders why he can't get rid of them. He's afraid she won't write to him again; he's afraid that she will.

Then, on a rainy morning in April, as he and Mayling pack for their Lake District wedding:

04-03-03
6:31 pm (GMT +7)

Dave, this is me saying hi/bye before I take off, but also to tell you I had the craziest dream last night and you were in it! You're in Hong Kong for just one day and we meet in this empty café in TST, on a little side street away from the tourists. I order a pork chop sandwich and I'm drinking tea in this thick white cup. You ask me if it's Hong Kong coffee tea, the kind with carnation milk and paint stripper strength that gives you a paranoid caffeine buzz for the next six hours. I say yes it is and you say, "I don't know how you can drink that. Looks like well-blended diarrhea." And then I say, "I like this shit," and that makes you laugh. Then I tell you about my plan to quit my job to make a documentary.

You say, "What's it about? Death rites, something like that?"

I say, "No, it's about dancing. I want to talk to people about the trancey state you can reach where you don't think about anything. I'm going to start in India. I'm also thinking about Bavaria. Spain. Probably Texas, too. I visited my friend in the States and saw line-dancing for the first time and it was so uplifting. I liked the synchronicity and the feeling of community."

You say, "Sounds trememdous. I heard that line-dancing is for people who have no imagination."

You're being mean and you don't sound like you. I tell you I'm sorry for not writing sooner and that I understand why you'd be pissed about it. You sigh. "I'm not. You seem well, and I'm happy for you, honestly. And I think it's great, your little dance movie idea."

I laugh. "You can't help yourself, can you?"

"No." You take a sip from my tea. You screw up your face in disgust as you return the cup to its saucer. "I can't help myself."

Freaky, huh? So anyway, I really am taking off to do my little dance movie, in exactly twenty-four hours in fact. My uncle and aunts insisted on a send-off, so we had a barbecue yesterday at Aunt Mei's cottage on the river. It's the first time I've seen everyone in months, and it's beautiful: sky and mountains all around and green, green fields. We sit around the barbecue pit, my uncle and aunts and cousins, roasting meat and fish over white-hot coals. Aunt Mei fusses over me, insists I don't have enough mosquito spray on and pushes the aerosol into my hands. Aunt Flora's dishing out her homemade sweet rice soup. Did I tell you her husband screwed around, went bankrupt, and left her with loan sharks graffiting threats over the front of her apartment? Now she's an obsessive angler. She sits in a boat on a lake in the middle of nowhere with her fishing rod and a floppy sun hat and stays there for hours. I think it calms her.

Uncle Yun tells me about wanting to get out of electronics, maybe opening up a café instead. He's also started Korean classes. He's a little bit shy and a little bit proud when he demonstrates the few phrases he can say: Hello. How are you. Would you like some tea.

I look at them all, and I think: We're showing each other so much love. But see what it took...

So the sun is setting, I've got a million mosquito bites on my legs, and I'm getting on a plane tomorrow. I have my passport, ticket, and $$$. Adios my friend, and thank you and good luck with everything. See you in the next life. // Yi

Dave decides he will write a proper reply, a decent one, in which he will wish her well and tell her that he is all right, too, he really is—but he will need to think carefully before he does this. He is afraid that a stupid comment or question might upset the happiness that she seems to have found, even though she still sounds a little desperate. He will have to think a bit about what to say, and when he does think of it, he will write. But part of him suspects that in the end he will leave it too long and the moment will have passed and he will not write after all.

In the meantime, he marries Mayling in a small chapel in the Lake District. Afterwards they have a modest reception in the village hall. Scottish salmon and Cava champagne is served to their sixty guests, which consists of twenty-one people on Dave's side and thirty-nine on Mayling's, including her parents, who've flown in from the States and comment on how small everything is. There is dancing (Sade, Prince, Al Green, Barry White...) and a brief, humorous speech by Nathan, his best man. Five days later they have a banquet in Hong Kong. Four hundred and fifty guests pull up at round tables in the Marriott Hotel ballroom; each table has a different floral centerpiece and is named accordingly on the seating plan (Baby's Breath, Daisy, Rose...). The guests drink Moet champagne and work through an eighteen-course dinner. Mayling and Dave visit each table and toast the guests, who toast them back and force them to drink tumblers of XO brandy (Mayling does Dave's share of the drinking). Dave and Mayling give short, carefully rehearsed speeches from the stage, in which they thank God and everyone they know.

There are games. In one game, Dave and Mayling have to roll an orange back and forth between themselves three times without using their hands. In another game, Mayling ties a napkin around her eyes for a blindfold. Four male guests are invited up to the stage and stand in a line with Dave. In this game, the bride is led to each male guest, who kisses her on the cheek. Afterwards she must try to guess which of the five males is her husband. The first in line is a plump man in his fifties whom Dave recognizes as a distant uncle. As Mayling offers her cheek, Dave imagines the future children he will have with her: a boy and a girl, he decides, both of them absurdly bright and good-looking. He imagines family walks in the country, Mayling telling them about different trees and birds and flowers. It will be unbearably happy.

Mayling offers her cheek to the next in line, a boy of three. As his mother lifts him up to kiss her and the room applauds and laughs, Dave imagines their children growing up and leaving home, and he wonders if they'll be glad and relieved and as full of resentment as he once was, and whether they'll think to call him when he needs them to, when he is old and alone in a room perhaps. Then he imagines that Mayling will outlive him, which means that she will be the one who is old and alone in a room, and this thought suddenly seizes him with fear and sadness. He will let her be the favorite parent, the funny one who listens and lets the kids break the rules a little, if that's what it'll take to get a phone call. If this doesn't work and they still don't call, and he's definitely sure he's going to go before her—say, a doctor has given him two months to live—maybe he'll have to kill her and then kill himself. Yes, he thinks. I could do that. Mayling offers her cheek to him. Dave leans in and kisses it. Her skin is warm; it smells heavy with perfume, brandy, and fatigue.

She touches his arm. "It's you, isn't it?"

Dave looks at his wife, who is smiling under her napkin blindfold, and he nods.

"It's me."

A REASONABLE PERSON

WITH ALMOST TWO HOURS to spare until the Hung Shing Plastics anniversary dinner, and with the hotel crawling with sweaty executives and managers (they are everywhere—the lobby, the bar, in elevators and corridors), the young couple in 501 decide to hide in their room until they are required to join the others in the Grand Ballroom.

They make use of the time. They strip down to their underwear and watch the first half of a TV documentary on pandas, make love, and play eight rounds of gin rummy (she carries a deck of cards whenever they travel). The husband, feeling badly about attending his company dinner on their one-year anniversary, deliberately loses the last five games. He does his punishment of ten push ups, the last five with a hand behind his back. She applauds and he gives a theatrical bow and retreats to the bathroom, where he starts running a shower.

When her husband emerges from the bathroom, she says, "How was your shower?" and he says, "Too wet," and she laughs. She changes into one of the dresses she has brought on this trip and smooths down the sides as she turns left and right in the mirror. She straightens her husband's tie and they go down to the ballroom, where most people have already found their seats. A speech, some awards. A slide presentation on the new factory site. The president feigns disappointment that the dinnerware is not made of plastic, a joke he's apparently made at all of the previous anniversary dinners. Food. Alcohol. Dancing. Tired from wine and small talk, she excuses herself at an acceptable hour and stumbles up to the room, where she falls into a restless sleep. Some time later her husband comes in, warm and heavy from brandy.

Under the dark, moonlit chandelier, they work to ignore the sticky heat, trying different ways to be together so that no gaps are left unclosed. The room is high-ceilinged with a paradise mural whose curling vines lurk and spread like shadows across the walls. The sparkling, constant purr of cicadas pours in from a nearby field. The two of them pull closer in the half-dark. The bed feels so large it makes her think of a raft floating on a lake.

For several hours she dreams of nothing, then apples. Later, in the dark, she awakes feeling thirsty and a little hungry. She thinks of the kettle somewhere in the room and fruit in a basket that had been left on the side table. Instead of getting up straight away, she decides to lie there for a moment as she watches the moonlight and vines and shadows swimming about the room, the chandelier above them shimmering quiet. She thinks, *This is what it means to be happy. I am happy.* Before her husband, she had never been on a plane, never stayed in a hotel; in fact, she used to clean rooms like this with her mother. She wonders why she feels this obligation to cherish the moment, and she knows it is because she imagines that, like all good things, it might not last. This takes away a little of her happiness.

And she is still thirsty, thirstier than before. She is thirstier than she is happy, and this does not seem right to her. She is lying very close to her husband, his skin warm and breathing. She wants very much to pull him closer and wrap her arms around his chest and squeeze him, but she is afraid to wake him. For a while she does nothing except observe the tiny, cool gaps where their bodies can't meet. But the longer she observes, the more gaps she finds, and the more unhappy she becomes. By this time she is more unhappy than she is happy, but as long as she is thirstier than she is unhappy, things might still be all right. She decides she should stop thinking about the gaps where she and her husband cannot meet and try instead to relax and observe the moonlight, the swimming shadows, the way they reached for each other in the night, the chandelier shimmering silently above them.

The room passes into darkness. Then the moon returns and the chandelier crystals catch the light and swallow it whole.

One crystal, hanging on the outer edge, mesmerizes her. When she tilts her head a little in one direction, the crystal throws out a sharp, alarming light. Another way and it slips into dark. Another way and she sees the extraordinary light trapped inside, cool, glowing, pulsing.

Slowly she peels her arm from under her husband's, feeling moist stickiness and then a light cooling on her skin. Blood rushes back into her limb. He turns away, taking some of the sheet with him. She slips out from the covers, tip-toes to the foot of the bed, and stands under the chandelier. Her hands find the hard back of a chair and she pulls it towards her and climbs onto it. It wobbles a little under her. She stands up slowly, and then, with careful fingers, reaches up for her crystal, unhooking it and bringing it to her chest. It is bumpy and cool. She opens her palm and stares at the dark thing. Then she looks up and sees that there are many more, all still glowing. She reaches up again, toward the middle this time, and plucks out a smaller one, then another, then another, until they almost spill from her hand and chest and there is nothing left to do but stand there, slightly elated, cradling her bounty. The pieces of blunt, warm glass begin sticking to her skin.

She imagines herself then—naked, on a badly made chair, dismembering a chandelier—and her skin starts to tingle with shame. Slowly she climbs down. She takes the chandelier pieces and lays them on the carpet under the bed. Then she sits in the chair with her hands in her lap and thinks about how, compared to when she first awoke, she probably does not have that much happiness left.

And her body has not forgotten: she is thirsty still, thirstier than before. She wants water so badly. Surely it is all right to want that? She can go to the kettle and pour herself a glass. But she notices that even now her thirst is still greater than her unhappiness, and as long as this is true, she might be okay.

When her husband does finally stir, the room is bright with morning. His face is pale, squashed from sleep, his features soft and blurred. He yawns and sees her sitting in the chair and says, "What are you doing over there, Mei?"

His hair is sticking up at the back like a duckling's tail. He looks somehow younger, and there is a question in his eyes, almost helpless or expecting, as if he knows she's been leading a secret life and is waiting for a confession.

And she replies: "Nothing. I just got up. Want some coffee?"

She goes over to him and kisses him on his forehead. While he is in the shower, she drinks five glasses of water, and after that she gathers up the chandelier pieces, gets back on the chair, and one by one hooks them back into place. All except for one.

Later that morning, sitting next to her husband on the flight back to Hong Kong, she drinks an orange juice and clutches her head during the descent. She reaches into her pocket and squeezes the crystal, digging its edges into her flesh. She thinks of an apple being slowly peeled. Then she thinks of bolts of silk spilling out with quick drama. She tells herself that somehow it will happen, it *must* happen: a time when she will be able to tell someone everything, and not want or fear anything.

ACCIDENT

THE DRIVER IS TAKING polaroids of the damage to his car, to the other car. He has good insurance. It is night and raining. He walks around the scene, not paying much attention to the shattered glass all around, or to the large, ugly punch in the side of his Benz. He isn't aware of the stickiness on his temple or the old woman fussing over her husband, who is sitting on the curb with his hand on his head. He isn't thinking about the meeting he was rushing to that he will now be very late for. And he has forgotten entirely about the sweat rings under his armpits that moments before had concerned him deeply. His preoccupation is with the one car window that hasn't been damaged. It is on the front passenger side, where his sister once sat and tried to talk to him. And as he stops to touch the glass that is strong, intact, and glistening with condensation trails, he is suddenly angry. The realization that he won't make it—that the trauma to his head will lead to a hemorrhage that will eventually kill him—that is part of it. But mostly he is angry because he despised his sister, and yet she has come to him now, and he can't find her face or name, or understand his desire to remember the things she once said.

I HAVE NEVER PUT
MY HOPE IN ANY
OTHER BUT THEE

WE WERE ALMOST AT the entrance of Matilda Hospital when Vivienne announced that she'd changed her mind. She said she would get something for my father after all, and despite my protests, she instructed Keung, our driver, to turn the car around and take us all the way back down the hill and through the Cross Harbor tunnel traffic to Kowloon, where he was to drop us off on the steps of Tiffany & Co.

Vivienne and my father should not have lasted this long. They married six weeks after meeting at a charity gala, and somehow, almost a year later, they were still together, even though it seemed to me that they'd spent much of that time arguing. Most of their arguments were about spending: how much time he spent away on business, how much money she spent on herself (she'd taken over the guest room with her winter clothes and filled the upstairs bathroom with her shoes and antique vases). Their arguments were tenaciously mobile; if one started in the kitchen, it would continue up the staircase, through the bathroom, the bedroom, the upstairs study. If they brought the argument into my immediate proximity—outside my bedroom door, or to the kitchen table, where I often did my homework—I'd turn up the volume on my headphones until they went away.

Now, as Keung drove us back towards Kowloon, Vivienne admitted tearfully to me that she felt responsible for my father's ulcer, and the ulcer before that. I said nothing to reassure her. She was in one of those moods where she wanted to indulge in her guilt. However, I knew that my father would never in fact give her full credit for the ulcer, would likely attribute it instead to the general stress of having to yell at his employees every day. He was a yeller, my father. He yelled at people's foolishness, at their lack of initiative, their blazing incompetence. He yelled when he didn't get his way. Nagging women, a badly made chair—these things also made him yell. But he never yelled at me.

Although the store was overwhelmed with Christmas shoppers, the young male clerk remained in sole attendance to us—to *her*—pulling out trays of gold, silver, diamonds. Vivienne stood tall and erect, a red cashmere shawl draped over her elegant cream suit. She frowned and shook her head at the clerk's offerings, an unhappy queen. Now and then I wandered off into the crowd or to different parts of the store in an attempt to alleviate my boredom (and to make my boredom known to Vivienne). But before too long I would be on tiptoe, peering over shoulders to see if she needed me.

Unlike most of the girls I knew, I took an odd sort of pride in making myself look as basic and graceless as possible. (That morning I'd slouched down the stairs in a wrinkled Clash t-shirt and a grubby pair of jeans. Vivienne had pressed her lips together and exhaled thinly before summoning herself to a state of acceptance. "Are you sure you'll be warm enough?" was all she would say.) I didn't care for pretty things, but there was something about the diamond swans in one of the display cabinets in the store. I pressed my fingertips against the glass and watched the cluster of cygnets turning slowly on the carousel. I fixed on their hard, diamond bodies, trying to push my gaze to their center, but they were too densely cut, their infinite passages and dispersions of light too complex for the human eye. I was jealous of light.

"AUDREY! AUDREY MA! OVER HERE!"

Heads turned, startled smiles. Vivienne had a penetrating soprano voice that had once filled opera houses. In a past life she had been a Musetta, a Cio-Cio San, and a Turandot. Now she was just Vivienne. Head low, frowning, I walked over to her with my hands shoved into my pockets.

"Audrey, you have a good eye. Tell me what you think of these."

Vivienne had recently come to believe that I possessed the soul of an artist. The previous semester, I'd represented my high school in a painting competition. My art teacher had submitted a piece I'd made for class, an abstract expressionist reworking of a Ch'ing dynasty landscape in winter. I'd spilled some paint on a canvas, then, as a joke, added some realist pandas chewing on bamboo shoots in the foreground. The piece ended up winning first prize and had been exhibited for five days in a student show at the Hong Kong Arts Center. From that point on, according to Vivienne, I was an artist, with a good eye. Vivienne had excitedly bought me a stack of large, glossy art books and an assortment of supplies—drawing pads, paints, an easel, canvases of various sizes—that sat in a corner of my room in their plastic wrappings like mummies waiting to reanimate. Every week or so she'd ask me over breakfast, *Anything inspire you lately?* I'd shrug and shake my head, mutter something about schoolwork. Whenever she turned her hopeful gaze on me, my body would warm and quiver with a shame I couldn't comprehend.

"Mrs. Ma."

The sales clerk presented the cufflinks on a plump display cushion. They were square and thick and made of sterling silver.

"Well?" said Vivienne. "What do you think?"

A crab was engraved on each one. Too cute. It didn't matter anyway. My father had a million cufflinks and wore none of them. My feet hurt.

"Why *crabs?*" I asked.

Vivienne stiffened a little. "I thought they were charming. And your father *is* a Cancer."

"A fine choice for a birthday or a Christmas gift," said the clerk. (The gold pin on his lapel flashed as he moved. Vincent Liu, Sales Executive. He was not too much older than me, maybe nineteen or twenty. Pale and sort of dreamy looking. He had an air of seeming completely unaware of his charms, which I found deeply appealing, though I doubted anyone had that kind of innocence.)

My stepmother smiled and shook her head. "It's just a gift."

"Well, your husband's a lucky man."

It was an obvious line, but Vincent Liu said it gently, in a way that seemed genuine and even a little regretful. He had such a nice voice. . .maybe he did mean it. It was time to leave. I picked up one of the cufflinks and pretended to inspect it.

"Nice," I said to Vivienne. "You should get them."

"Really? You think your father will like them?"

"Yeah, he'll love them."

Vivienne handed over her credit card.

"Your daughter has good taste," he smiled.

Neither of us bothered to correct him. We had become used to it by then. The first time someone had mistaken us for mother and daughter was at a Jockey Club benefit we'd gone to with my father. He had bumped into a former school friend whom he hadn't seen in years. My father had introduced us—*my wife, my daughter*—at which the friend had exclaimed with practiced sincerity that surely Vivienne was too young to be my mother, that we must be sisters. Vivienne humored him well enough, chatting merrily while I scowled at the idiot, wanting to set him straight. My father stopped me. Not with anything that he said, but with his face, which was frozen in an embarrassed rictus grin that I hadn't seen before or since. It was as if he'd never considered the inevitability of such a misunderstanding, and now that it had occurred, he was incapable of locating the words that would carry truth.

Later that night, Vivienne and I crossed paths on the moonlit stairs at home with drinks in our hands.

"Thirsty?" she asked, looking at my glass of water.

I nodded. She held her own glass up in sympathy, though I knew hers wasn't water. I'd heard their voices earlier, and I could smell the angry sourness on her breath. Then she said that people in general had an odd, lazy compulsion to join up the dots. She claimed, with a wave of her hand, that she really didn't mind at all if I wanted to set people straight and tell them she wasn't actually my mother. I replied with a shrug that I really couldn't be bothered with what other people thought. She accepted my response with a civil nod, and without saying goodnight, turned down the hall to the room where she and my father slept. We never spoke about it again. But that night, as I got back into bed and pulled the covers around me, I thought how, despite what she'd said, telling the truth would probably hurt her feelings just a little.

We walked a block to the Peninsula Hotel and waited for Keung. Vivienne had instructed him to keep circling until she called him to pick us up. This seemed reasonable enough; parking was difficult in that area, and we were only making a quick stop. I suspected, however, that Vivienne had given him these instructions because she didn't like the idea of our driver not driving. One afternoon she'd seen him dozing with a newspaper spread over the dashboard. She'd turned to me and said, "Well, what do you think of *that*." I'd reasoned that Keung was almost sixty and still getting up at five every morning to take me to school; it was natural that he would get a little tired in the afternoon. I had always been fond of Keung, I told her. He had a gentle, steady way about him and had been with us forever. "A bit too long if you ask me," Vivienne had replied.

Despite the cool wind sweeping in from the harbor, she decided we would wait outside the entrance. We looked out onto the hotel's large, oval forecourt with its pruned hedges and ornate centerpiece: a thick, gushing fountain with dolphins frozen mid-leap. Beyond that were the Salisbury Road shoppers moving in distracted patterns, inadvertently hitting prams and dogs with their oversized shopping bags. Further down were the harbor waters, dense green-brown and full of metal and contaminated marine life that nonetheless got pulled up like prizes by the amateur anglers lining the waterfront promenade. Across the harbor was Hong Kong Island, with its cramped skyline of paranoid, competing neon brands. The Bank of China building rose up like a dark knife, its white crosses giving off bad chi to its neighbors. And beyond that was the winding green Peak Road, at the top of which my father lay in a stiff bed in a bright, air-conditioned hospital room. I imagined him alone there, dumb and startled, in a scratchy gown that irritated and embarrassed him.

"Let's go for afternoon tea after we see your father," suggested Vivienne. "We haven't done that in a such a long time."

I gestured at the ugly block of beige across the road. "I have to go to the Museum of Art, remember?"

"Oh?" She smiled. "What are you going to do there?"

"Look at art, I guess." I caught the meanness in my voice. I tried again. "Miss Lin—"

"Your art teacher?"

"Yeah. She gave us an assignment to complete over the Christmas break. We have to choose a piece of art and write a page about it." I sighed. "If it's a Chinese piece, the paper has to be written in English. Anything else has to be written in Chinese."

Vivienne seemed amused by the idea. "I think I'll join you."

I shrugged. The truth was that I actually didn't mind having someone with me on what had promised to be a tedious chore.

"Good. We'll do that first, then the hospital. Don't worry, we'll have plenty of time for your father."

"Are you sure? What about Keung? He's coming to pick us up, isn't he?"

"I'll call him." She held her cell phone to her ear and smiled reassuringly. "Don't worry. I'll take care of it."

I had to admit that it made sense logistically to go to the museum first. We crossed the road and walked through the courtyard with its Indian fortune tellers and imported palm trees. For a while we stood in the lobby, pondering the program board, which displayed information about the museum's permanent collection of Asian art as well as a special exhibition of international art.

"I don't know if I want to write the essay in Chinese or English," I said sulkily. Sometimes I hated the sound of my voice, and I could tell Vivienne didn't like it either.

"Well," she said. "I suggest we walk about and see what inspires you. How does that sound?"

"Okay. But we shouldn't stay too long."

We took the escalator to the upper floors and worked hastily through "The Unrestrained Brush: Selections from the Xubaizhai Collection of Chinese Calligraphy II" and "Metal, Wood, Water, Fire, and Earth: Gems of Antiquity." Vivienne started reminiscing about the the Vermeers she'd seen at the Royal Academy, so we moved down to the next floor to "International Art Through the Ages."

The exhibition was screened off into four separate rooms, displaying paintings from different movements and periods, while sculptures from the same period were dotted around the remaining space without much consideration. We shared a vaguely similar route through the exhibition, Vivienne moving with slow, measured purpose while I slouched a little behind or hurried ahead, stretching my arms up or folding them or stuffing my hands in my pockets. At one point I left Vivienne with a landscape while I studied a bronze sculpture in the next room of a giant man in mid-stride. He looked sort of compressed, as if he'd been whittled down to his bare essence, a rough, unfinished look to his surface. As I came closer, his features began to lose their defining edges, appearing to dissolve into a knobbly surface of waves, knots, and twists. I stepped back a few feet and saw that it was still a man. I amused myself with this for a while, coming close then stepping back, experimenting with distance, trying to find the point where the column of metal no longer resembled a man, dissolving instead into texture and form. When this became tiresome, I decided to look for Vivienne.

I found her in the last room, looking at a painting of a dark-haired woman in a white Victorian dress. The woman was standing tall and erect, a pale hand resting on the back of a stiff, plum-colored chair. She had a thin nose, and her small lips were pressed into a heart shape. Looking at the slender line of Vivienne's profile, I saw then how still and pale she was, the composed readiness of her smile. I read the plaque and found out that the woman in the painting was an English duchess. I relayed this information to Vivienne.

"Does that mean she's royalty?" I asked.

"Hmmm. . ." Vivienne squinted, looking closer at the painting, as if the answers were to be found in the brushwork or a detail of lace. The duchess retained her composure under the scrutiny. Vivienne stepped back at last from the painting, regarding it with an odd, mesmerized sort of gaze.

"Did you find anything to write about?" she asked.

"What? Oh, I don't know. Maybe. Yes. I think I've got enough notes," I lied. I hadn't taken any notes. As usual, nothing had sustained my interest, and as usual I was lazily confident that I'd be able to come up with something at the last minute. "It's almost four. We should probably go, shouldn't we?"

"Yes, I suppose we should."

As we took the escalator down to the lobby, Vivienne complained about the poor lighting in all the exhibitions and the carpeting in the Asian Art room.

"Art and carpets," she declared, crossing the lobby floor. "*No.*"

As we walked towards the exit, Vivienne noticed a set of double doors to our left.

"Oh, I wonder what's in there," she said, already walking towards it.

"Vivienne," I protested. "Dad will be waiting." I stopped a moment, then decided to catch up.

Standing side by side, we peered in through the row of small glass panes set in the top halves of the doors and saw a large, white space. We entered the room, gravely silent. A parade of black floor-standing speakers formed a circle around the room's perimeter. I noticed that there were breaks in the circle after every five speakers. There were eight breaks. Forty speakers total. A comfortable-looking bench stood in the center of the space. Vivienne and I lingered by the doors, uncertain. We decided the exhibition was probably still in preparation, but as we turned to leave, the room started humming with sound. Startled, our eyes darted around. No. It was just the two of us. We smiled at each other, confused and a little embarrassed. Vivienne checked the sign by the door. *Forty Part Motet (2001). Sound installation.* Her expression relaxed into recognition, and she gestured to the speakers.

"They're preparing," she said triumphantly.

"They? Who?"

"The choir," she smiled, still pleased with herself.

A disembodied male voice—Vivienne told me it was the choirmaster—issued vague instructions in English. Somewhere to our left we heard the chit-chat of awaiting singers. We began walking around the space, investigating, eavesdropping. We leaned into one loudspeaker and heard a bass clear his throat of phlegm. A tenor two places down from him said, *"I didn't quite hear that properly."* Laughter. A boy soprano in an affected voice said *"and this is Spem in Alium by Thomas Tallis... la di da..."* A baritone practiced his scales. And further down:

"Do you mind passing this to Stafford?"

"I'm not touching that."

"What about you?"

"Which one's Stafford?"

"Oscar Wilde. Bass-baritone."

The tap of a conductor's baton ordered the room into silence. Vivienne took hold of my arm and led me to the center of the room.

"Close your eyes."

"What? Why?"

"Trust me. Close your eyes..." She looked terribly excited.

I shrugged my shoulders, and she squeezed my arm, approving. When I closed my eyes, the weight of her touch disappeared. The air was cold on my lips.

A solitary voice, mournful and androgynous, swept over my shoulder and began spiraling skywards. Suddenly my skin was tingling warm. Now a second voice came, lower, as if it were falling down a well. Then another, again deep...then another, this one higher: four voices, then six, eight—they were coming too quickly, multiplying, thickening, holding for so long it seemed almost inhuman. The voices broke off, then quickened in swarms, soaring, spiraling, driving down into depths, circling and crossing, fading, diving, gently bearing down…conspiracies of whispers that teased close then vanished, only to return again, sometimes consoling, sometimes mocking, sometimes pitying… why pitying? Pitying *me*? A terrific rising, a monstrous wave—

I opened my eyes.

The circle of black speakers looked newly ominous as the ghost choir continued singing, flooding the room. I felt dull, heavy, my mind alert only to the cold sheen on my skin and the thick, slow swirling in my chest. Vivienne stood a few feet away, eyes closed, an expression of astonished pleasure on her face. I started towards her, then stopped. I wasn't afraid of disturbing her; rather, a strange certainty fell upon me that even if I were to touch her arm or try to speak to her, she would not know I was there.

Vivienne found me later sitting on the floor by the doors outside the exhibition room.

"There are chairs everywhere, Audrey. What are you doing down there?"

I got up off the floor and busily straightened myself.

"Oh," she said, turning to the door. "I think they're starting again." She was looking through the glass panes. An old man with powdery white hair sat on the bench, his tweed shoulders trembling like a moth.

"What's wrong with him?" I asked.

Vivienne didn't answer. She was humming to the music, eyes half-closed.

"He's not crying, is he?"

Vivienne turned to me with a beatific smile. "See how music can touch the soul?" She touched my arm. "Look. You have goose bumps, too."

I looked at the pin-sized bumps along my forearm.

"I'm just cold, that's all."

I saw her stiffen. I knew I'd hurt her. I couldn't bear her hope for me. I wanted to crawl away unnoticed. She wanted me to say, *Yes, I felt it too. I know exactly what you mean.* But I was quite certain that what I had experienced was not transcendence. I had felt dizziness and nausea. Nothing like the way she'd looked, that foreign expression of ecstasy that had felt too intimate to witness.

"Sorry." I'd sneezed on her. I started wiping her jacket with my sleeve, but she waved me away.

"Just clean up your nose. Take one of these." She pulled two tissues out of her purse, one for me and one for herself. As she carefully dabbed at her jacket, I could see that she was trying to manage a smile, but the effort made her look sad and a little exasperated. I said again that I was sorry.

"All right, Audrey," she said, not looking at me as she pressed the tissue against her sleeve. "Never mind."

We sat silently as the car climbed the steep, winding hill to Matilda Hospital, the crab cufflinks nestled snugly inside a small box wrapped in silver (not by Vincent Liu, not that I cared, but I still made sure I was the one who held it). With each bend and curve we left a little more of the city behind. Blotchy, low-rise apartment complexes and glowing supermarkets and filling stations gave way to lines of close, bending trees; a small, grey-tiled school for girls; a Spanish-style villa behind iron gates; more conspiratorial trees. The low engine drone made my skin hum and sent strange signals to my brain. We took another bend and passed a jogger, a fair Caucasian man in a t-shirt and thick white trainers. We took another bend and saw a young Filipina maid being pulled uphill by a large, salivating Doberman. We took another bend. My head felt muddy, and that dreadful swirling started again in my chest. I felt sick and sorry for myself.

The old man had cried. And Vivienne, she'd looked...transported. How many other people had felt whatever she'd felt? And how many had just felt odd, or nothing at all? My nausea worsened, and I squeezed the little box. I wanted a gentle hand on my head and a voice telling me everything was okay, that this feeling would pass. Vivienne's head was turned to the window. A dark, subdued mass of hair, a swan neck. She was contemplating the trees perhaps, or the sky losing its light. I looked at the back of Keung's head. It was grey, silent. Are we there yet? I wanted to speak, to hear my voice, any voice. But I also had a strange conviction that the silence was holding us all together.

I turned the silver box over in my hand, feeling a little bad for the crabs. They would never find their way onto a shirt cuff. Best to stay inside. I wondered what my father would be like at the hospital this time, if he'd be a little bit more cooperative. When I'd gone there to see him for the first ulcer, I'd heard yelling as soon as I'd stepped out of the elevator. A pair of young nurses were gossiping loudly at the desk about how impossible the patient was being, demanding to be let out early, absolutely had to be in New York by Tuesday. Apparently, though, Dr. Chan was having none of it. I walked down the hall to my father's room and waited outside for a few minutes, listening to him and the doctor have it out. It sounded like fun. Eventually Dr. Chan came out—a broad, pinkish man—looking harassed but somewhat pleased with himself.

I knew being confined to a hospital bed was torture for my father. He liked to be on the move all the time. "There goes the Great White Shark"—that was what Vivienne would say whenever he would go off on another one of his business trips to Tokyo, San Francisco, London. In the beginning, she went with him, but she quickly realized that she'd see little more of him than if she stayed behind in Hong Kong. It seemed to me that my father spent more time in the air, crossing continents and time zones, than here on the ground with the rest of us. Now and then, though, when he was home for a brief spell between trips, he might notice me at the kitchen table with my homework scattered about, and he'd pull up a chair (but not sit in it) and shake his newspaper open and make some sort of comment about how disappointing the world was, or how this political party or that industrial sector needed to get its act together. I'd nod or shrug as if I knew exactly what he meant, responding at appropriate moments to his weary tirade while pretending to work on algebra or French participles. As soon as I put my pencil down, he'd say he was interrupting my studies and disappear for another week. At the time, it didn't seem strange to me that these were the moments we spent together.

"You look like you're going to be sick."

"What?" I looked at Vivienne, who was frowning at me, then at Keung, who was still driving.

"You look like you're going to be sick."

"No, I'm fine."

"We can stop."

"No, it's okay."

"We'll stop." Vivienne leaned forward. "Stop the car, driver."

"I can't stop here, Mrs. Ma," said Keung.

"If you don't stop, she's going to throw up."

Keung didn't respond straight away. "There's a rest area," he said. "It'll be another few minutes. I can stop there, but not—"

"Fine, fine." Vivienne waved her hand and sat back in her seat. She gave me a satisfied, reassuring sort of smile. I looked away, embarrassed for her, ashamed of myself. I wanted to tell her that she shouldn't speak to Keung like that, but I didn't. I was suddenly afraid she would leave us.

We pulled over along the hiker's trail. At first Keung kept the engine running, but Vivienne told him to turn it off. She and I walked a little way down the road to the vista point. On a balding patch of grass next to a sign asking people not to litter stood a metal bench that had been painted bright green. A plastic rail ran along the side of the hill. Another sign: No Climbing. We sat next to each other on the bench and looked down at the city. Millions of edges, grey, blue and white. Some early lights. I felt a little sleepy and leaned lightly against Vivienne's arm. Her shawl tickled my cheek.

"We're in a black and white movie," I said, yawning.

"Oh it's not that bad," she mused, though I hadn't meant it like that. "It actually reminds me of English weather. Everyone complains about it being grey all the time, but once you get used to it. . ." She searched for the words. "It has an almost grudging kind of beauty, if that makes any sense."

"It's so grey," I nodded sleepily.

"And so *defiant* in its greyness," she said. "After a while, you can't help but appreciate its conviction." I heard satisfied amusement in her voice.

"It *is* pretty," I murmured.

We sat for some time, saying nothing. It got colder. A little more of the light left the city. Soon it had the hushed glow of old silver, like a weird treasure that has been locked away in a chest for decades. I turned to look at Vivienne, and in the bluish half-light she appeared softer, a little unformed. But more or less the same.

She asked me if I was feeling any better, and I said yes. She nodded, and we looked at the lights scattered over our darkening island for a while longer. Then she turned to me with a funny sort of smile.

"When your father gets angry—I mean, really angry—do you know what I do?"

I shrugged, but I knew. You shout. You scream. You start on the gin.

"I *laugh*. He hates it when I laugh at him. When I saw the crabs on those cufflinks, I almost died. Your father, when he gets really hot and bothered, his face turns bright red and he balls his hands into these pathetic little fists, and I can't help thinking of a crab thrashing about in a pot of hot water—"

She stopped herself then, and looked at me as if she had done me some terrible wrong.

"We ought to go," she said, getting up and straightening herself. As she smoothed the length of her shawl, she managed a smile, and before turning towards the path, she waved her palm at me as if beckoning a small child or a pet.

"Come now, Audrey," said Vivienne. "Visiting hours will be over soon."

WEDDING NIGHT

I.

ONE SUMMER MORNING, SING receives a visitor at the house. He greets her, "Big Sister Fong," then remains standing until she's seated. He offers her tea, which she accepts.

The living room is dim in the mornings. A lazy fly darts off the dining table. Fong sits in silence, waiting until the flask and cups have been set out. She notices the cups are cracked with use; strings of etched ghost leaves cling to their sides. She remembers these were a common design when she was a girl. At one point she'd had a set of six herself, but her husband had managed to break too many of them over the years. She must have replaced them. There is something touching and pitiful, she decides, about the way Sing hasn't thought to buy new ones.

"Ah Sing," she says, "this house must be a lot of work for one person. How do you find the time?"

Sing smiles a little. "Aside from letters and fishes, Big Sister Fong, I have little else to distract me."

He pours tea into his visitor's cup, then into his own. Steam ribbons upwards. Fong casts her gaze around the dark room, at the heavy, carved armchairs and the cabinets crammed with books and newspapers. It feels to her like a mausoleum.

"I'm sure your father would be touched that you've kept up the house so...faithfully," she says.

"Thank you."

"Most people expected you to run for election after he passed. He was a good village chief, but we all know how much you helped him."

Sing lays a finger on the rim of his cup. Fong brushes her fingertips against hers. "Ah! Ah!" she says, blowing on her hand.

"I'm sorry," says Sing. "I didn't think it would be too hot."

"Really," she says. She blows into the top of her cup and tries another sip. Still too hot. She smiles at her host.

"Let us talk frankly," she says. "You know my cousin has come back.

"I do."

"Three days now."

"Yes."

"Don't you want to see her? To know how she is?"

"It's been years."

"Exactly. Sing, let the past be past. For both your sakes."

There is something like a sudden deflation of the air between them.

"She's barely left the house since she returned." Fong's voice is softer now. "She recognizes her mistakes. If you want her, you may come by this evening for dinner. Make your intentions known then. There is no risk of disappointment, I can assure you."

A ring has been placed on the table between the two cups. It is gold, with a thick band of diamonds in the middle. Fong extends her finger and nudges it towards him.

"A token of sincerity," she says. "It was the first thing he bought her. Do with it as you please. I would guess that you'd want to bury it, but don't be ashamed to sell it. Others in your position would do the same. Besides, you know what happens to buried treasure around here—especially something like this." She is leaning towards the ring, and for a moment it seems as if she is about to pick it up again. However, she sits back. "He did very well for himself," she says, giving the ring a long, thoughtful look.

She doesn't notice Sing's reaction to her last remark, preoccupied as she is with considering her cousin's former suitor, his wealth and cunning, and how she, unlike her cousin, may have been able to overlook his cruelty. She takes another sip from her cup. Pleasantly hot. When she speaks again, there is some kindness in her expression.

"There's no shame in being practical." She smooths the wrinkles from her lap. "I'll be on my way. Thank you for the tea. No, don't get up. I'll see myself out."

II.

Wai Lan is bored at her cousin Fong's in the countryside, where she is to stay until her mother sends for her. She's been told all her life that she needs a firmer hand than her mother can give her. She's been called a devil running from fire—can't sit, can't wait, can't hear *no*.

Fong treats her well enough, but is twenty years her senior and full of seriousness, so Wai Lan feels they have little to talk about. Fong's husband is a neat, chubby man whom Wai Lan has caught staring at her on several occasions. His surname is Lam, and Wai Lan secretly calls him *Lam Bek Bek*—Softie Softie. Since injuring his back, he spends much of his time at home, so Wai Lan makes sure she does her chores quickly and is out of the house until her cousin returns from her secretarial job at the transport department. Most days, she wanders around the village looking for someone to chat with, or goes off on her own into the hills with a sun hat and a book. Sometimes she sits at a table outside the Brother Store, sipping on a soda or writing letters to her classmate Ga Ling, who lives on the same housing estate in the city as Wai Lan and her mother.

Wai Lan is writing to Ga Ling about the sunburn on her neck when she sees her elderly neighbour walk by with a large cardboard box.

"Can I help you with that box, grandmother?" she asks.

"Ha ha, didn't think you'd miss this," says the old woman, winking at her from under the brim of her wide bamboo hat. "Here, help me with the gate."

Wai Lan slides the metal latch and pushes the gate into the yard, letting the old woman through, then pushes it shut again from the inside.

"Let's have a look, then." The old woman sets the box down by the front door of her house and folds back the flaps. Wai Lan squats next to her and peers inside. The chicks are smaller than she imagined, no bigger than plums. She tries to count them, but they keep moving, hopping and tumbling into each other; she guesses fourteen. They are soft, furry balls of gold and chocolate brown.

"You'll eat three or four and keep the rest for eggs," Wai Lan guesses.

"Or give some away. Next time your mother comes to visit, ask if she'd like one for the Tuen Ng festival."

Wai Lan nods, her enthusiasm inspired less by the hope of pleasing her mother, or of eating juicy, steamed chicken, than by her desire right then to touch one of the creatures, to pick it up and let the warm thing sit in her curling palm. She runs a finger along its soft, flossy fur, feeling its tiny bones, all of its fragility in her hand.

Yes, she will leave and arrive in cities again and again, time passing through the wiping of tables, through cold apartment keys, kind strangers and broken sentences, afternoons wandering hungry through department stores, sandwiches with bad meat, dark guarded walks, the ecstasy of solitude, wishing the city would shake her, ignoring the more destitute, falling for black eyes, natural disasters, losing everything, café water that smells like sweat, letting the pile of dishes grow, lonely sex, adding deadbolts—

III.

Wai Lan's first interest beyond a boy—there had been many boys—had been Kwan Lau Ming, the young music teacher who'd been brought in to substitute for a month. It was April, but he wore a heavy three-piece suit. He was tall and his eyes were watery bright, the lashes almost girlish in their beauty. The students fell in love with him immediately, straightening their backs at the piano and pushing out their hopeful, adolescent chests for his attention. He gave them none, maintaining an expressionless reserve that his students decided was enigmatic. At the end of his final class, however, he'd made a point of speaking to Wai Lan.

"Miss Yip, " he said. "If you're interested, you can practice on the piano at my home."

"I can't afford private lessons," said Wai Lan.

"No charge," he said. He handed her a small piece of paper. "This is the address."

Wai Lan was intrigued by the fact that he added nothing more to his offer. He didn't try to convince her she had promising talent, or that it would help her failing grades. He didn't say that now that he had finished his post at the school he had more time on his hands and wanted to help out some of his less advantaged students. Whatever his reasons might have been, it seemed almost impolite to ask. And what could he really say?

So every Wednesday afternoon, she would go to his house and sit at his piano for an hour. He lived in a small apartment about a ten-minute walk from the school. The route took her past a tree-lined riverbank where her mother used to swim as a girl. Kwan Lau Ming would welcome her in, walk directly to the front room, and gesture to the upright piano against the wall. Wai Lan liked this room. It was modest and clean, full of neatly stacked paperbacks. The last fifteen minutes of the hour were her favorite; the windows would pull in the pinkish gold light of the evening sun, and she would now and again look up and see him standing over her, his suited shoulders at an angle, his eyes darkly shining in the dimming light.

One afternoon in June, Kwan Lau Ming told her they would have to stop the lessons. He had accepted a full-time teaching post in another district and would need the next few weeks to prepare for his move.

"You mean you'll have to give up this apartment?" said Wai Lan.

"Well yes, of course."

"I know it's a funny thing to say. It's just that I'll miss coming here. I never even got to see all of it."

"Oh?"

"Yes, I'm always just playing piano here in the front room. I've used the bathroom perhaps three times."

Kwan Lau Ming shrugged. "All right. Since it's your last lesson, I'll give you a guided tour."

He got up and opened a door to the right of the windows.

"Here's the kitchen. One stove ring, one pan—one of everything."

"Not even an extra set of chopsticks?" asked Wai Lan, peering round the doorframe at the pokey little room.

"No. There's the front room, which you're well acquainted with. And over there is the bathroom, which you're less well acquainted with, having used it only three times."

Wai Lan giggled.

"Well, I'm afraid this concludes our tour," he said, sitting down on the couch.

"Where do you sleep?" asked Wai Lan.

"Right here." He patted the arm of the couch as if it were a faithful dog. "The life of a poor teacher. It pulls out. That's where I lay awake at night, thinking…" He laughed a little, trailing off.

"What? What keeps you awake at night? Please, tell me." Wai Lan sat down next to him, folding her hands in the lap of her skirt.

Kwan Lau Ming hesitated, shook his head. "Just…I have these compositions. Good, bad, half-finished. A story you'll become familiar with."

"Oh," said Wai Lan. "Do you still write?"

"No. That's why I can't sleep."

"Oh…I see…"

"Don't worry, you're not supposed to have anything wise to say at—what are you, fourteen, fifteen?"

"Nearly fifteen. In August."

He laughed. "Fifteen in August. By then you'll have forgotten me anyway. It's just as well that I'm leaving."

"It's true," said Wai Lan.

"What is?"

"As you say, I'm just a kid. I'll find someone else to fixate on quickly enough."

Kwan Lau Ming clapped his hands and threw back his head in a throaty laugh that Wai Lan hadn't heard before. Suddenly she felt acute embarrassment at the hours she had spent playing so earnestly at his piano. She felt herself blushing and tugged the hem of her skirt at her knees.

"Let me tell you something," he said in a softer voice. "You never once asked me why I invited you here, or why you should come. You just came, played piano, and went home. You never brought it up. Not even today."

"No."

"You never needed me to tell you why. You made your own reason, Wai Lan. For that, you will always have my respect."

He leaned in, smoothing away some strands of hair that had fallen on her cheek. For the first time, she noticed there was no smell to him. His eyes were bright and shining with hunger.

Nobody looked up from their meals or their newspapers. They could not be pried from their dull serenity.

IV.

Wai Lan just happens to be passing by Sing's house as he returns from his rounds. Leaning on the metal gate, she introduces herself as Fong's cousin and asks if he has a letter for her. He says no, and she asks him what he's doing for the rest of the afternoon. When he tells her he's going fishing in the bay, she seems disappointed and announces that she'll occupy herself somewhere else then. But there she is the next day. This time she asks him what he hopes to catch, and he says, *Whatever wants to be caught*. As he goes inside, he thinks she is still at the gate looking at him. The day after that she is at the gate yet again, this time as he is leaving, and she invites herself along, asking does he mind, and he says fine, as long as she doesn't complain if she gets bored. And so she goes with him that day and the day after and the day after that.

At first she doesn't say much as she sits in the boat with him. (Years later, unable to maintain a clear memory of her face, he will carry in his head a bright landscape of sky and trees and the wide, still bay, disturbed only by the presence of a small boat and two blurry figures sitting in it, half obscured by the sunlight). Instead she trails her fingers in the water as he sings village songs in a low, humming voice. When she does begin to talk, she asks him how he learned to tie that funny knot, and what's the biggest fish he's caught, and has he ever loved anyone. He tries to answer her in a way that he hopes isn't too inviting or too dull. He can't tell if she's listening or not; oftentimes she'll be leaning over the boat edge, staring into the green water, her fist under her chin.

See the lush shouldered mountains, circled in a wide, silent meeting? See the scattering of iron masts poking at the blue sky? See the silhouettes of eagles arcing high over the village, where small figures move amongst furrows bursting with green? Where a sharp voice or a bicycle bell or even an insistent bee may fail to stir the dogs sleeping in their hot stone yards?

There are things she never tells him. That she saw him from the window and dreamed that night of chestnut skin. That she followed him through alleys and rice fields and up the dirt path that climbed the neck of the village, scurrying all the way and hiding a distance behind his steady, straight-backed walk. That when they are together she feels a fragile calm. That she sees the flickering uncertainty in his eyes as he considers her questions or when she attempts to answer those questions herself.

We meet for the first time so often that you're no longer you and I'm no longer much of me. Or maybe it's still us but slipped into new costumes that suit our new selves. You are more lost, more selfish. More slippery and brave. I am sometimes chasing, sometimes hiding. I give myself the things I never had, certain skills or education or clothes. I can't help putting a large window behind one of us.

She seems propelled by some unknown mission, one in which she has somehow decided he is her accomplice. Sometimes her eyes flash with jealousy when he mentions things she's never experienced or hasn't learned in school. She makes him sneak books from the schoolhouse or from his father's room for her. When the *Ming Pao* begins serializing *The Return of the Condor Heroes*, they spread the newspaper out on the blanket and read it together. Sometimes they read the stories aloud, though she prefers it when it isn't her turn. She says she likes his voice, but from her occasional hesitations before a word, he suspects that she is also a little self-conscious. When she does read, he rarely follows the story; instead he observes her slender stroke of body upon the blanket, her pale lick of nose, the steely quiet of her gaze. He wonders what dark gods of mischief have brought her to him.

V.

Wai Lan doesn't feel like going fishing. She expresses her desire for a bowl of sweet beancurd instead; it's the perfect thing, she says, to have on a hot afternoon. When she sees him hesitate, she sighs and places her hand on his arm.

"Just come and have a bowl with me, then you can go. I promise, the fish will not pine for you too much."

The two of them sit on the plastic stools at the Brother store in the shade, not noticing the lizard scurrying chaos in the dust around their feet. The owner sets the bowls of tofu down and holds up his hands when Sing tries to give him money, asking that he find out what's taking so long with the permits instead. Sing waves him away, muttering *okay, okay.*

"Together?" says Wai Lan, raising her spoon.

Sing waits for the owner to go back inside before acquiescing.

"Remember," she says, "no chewing on the first bite. One, two—"

They each put a spoonful into their mouths; the beancurd slips down their throats and sends a cold shiver down their spines.

"Good?"

"Good."

They eat in peaceful silence, heads bowed over their bowls.

She was sixteen. from the city. He'd thought at first it was a trifle, a foolish vanity, a fleeting, insubstantial attraction. *You mean,* she would say, *You thought I was a trifle, a vanity, insubstantial.*

He would later realize how mistaken he'd been about her; and she, over years, would impress upon him the extent of his mistake.

Digging her toes into the sand, Wai Lan gazes out into the distance at the coastline of Clearwater Bay. Beyond it is Ha Yeung Bay, and even farther out, the city. Sing shakes open the blanket and lays it on the sand.

"I'm glad to be far from home," she says.

He sets down the newspaper and a small bag of fruit. "Why *did* your mother send you here?"

Wai Lan grabs a handful of lychees. She brings one to her mouth and bites into the skin with a crack. "So sweet," she murmurs to herself. She eats another, then another, gazing out at the water. Then she spreads out the newspaper and turns the pages until she gets to the latest installment of *The Return of the Condor Heroes*. She beckons for him to join her, and they proceed to read in silence. Sing keeps losing his place, irritated by the wind rustling the pages and the constant crack of lychee skins.

"Big Sister Fong said you were put in her care," he says abruptly. "But you don't seem to need any looking after. She also said you were helping around the house, but that can't be true either."

"Why?"

"Well, you've been spending all your time with *me*."

Wai Lan thinks he's teasing, but sees that he isn't smiling.

"You're not complaining, are you?" she asks.

"You want me to guess your past offenses?" Sing shoots back.
He doesn't notice her wounded look, her face blooming with
tearful fury. He sees none of this. He's observing the specks of
sand that dot the discarded lychee skins, the fly that keeps darting
on then off, unable to make up its mind.

VI.

Upon her return to the city, Wai Lan finds things have changed. A thin, middle-aged man who sells insurance is lodging in her bedroom. Her mother tells her they need the extra income: she's hurt her wrist again and can't sew until she's recuperated. But Wai Lan finds it hard to suffer the man's wet, beady eyes staring at her across the dinner table, or the way her mother fawns over him in that embarrassing way of hers, her girlish laughter forced, her face too pale with powder, making her look like a ghost.

Wai Lan sleeps badly at night on the floor, the straw mat scratching her back, the insurance man passing her frequently on his way out to the shared toilet at the end of the hall. Wai Lan grows tired of pressing the pillow to her ear against the sound of water slapping the toilet and the slow-footed rhythm of the man's approach. After a month of this, she seeks out her old classmate Ga Ling.

For the past two months, Ga Ling has been working at the Fortune Star textile factory in Causeway Bay and renting a small apartment nearby that she can barely afford. It is draughty, the neighbors are loud, and every hard surface—the walls, the dresser, the window panes—is coated in a filmy grime that she tells Wai Lan isn't worth the trouble of cleaning as it all comes back after a few days. The girls put up a partition in the bedroom;

Ga Ling gets the half with the window. At night Wai Lan hears her friend's low, deep breathing through the board and smiles at the occasional laugh that bursts out of a dream. If she weren't so tired herself, she would slip into her friend's bed and hug her tight like a pillow.

Sing sleeps badly, and starts passing late, humid hours stationed at his bedroom window in a wooden chair salvaged by his father. By draping his forearms over its thin, sloping arm rests and barely moving, he can sit for long periods of time without getting too hot or sweaty. He might resemble a prisoner awaiting interrogation or execution, but he finds that if he's able to maintain enough composure, he actually starts to cool down. Even so, he can't sleep.

To help with rent, Wai Lan quits school and goes to work with Ga Ling at the factory where, for eleven hours a day, five to six days a week, they sit at weaving looms in a large, hot room with thirty other workers. A sign on the wall reads "No Loud Talking," and they have to raise their hand for permission to use the toilet, which they must limit to two visits per shift. For each additional visit, their pay will be docked by five percent.

At the end of the work day, Wai Lan and Ga Ling hurry arm in arm along the dark roads back to their apartment, where they share a meager dinner and a cigarette. Once a week, they wash themselves at the bathhouse.

"You're so lucky," whispers Wai Lan, admiring her friend's figure as she lowers herself into the water.

"You mean these?" smiles Ga Ling, cupping her breasts.

"All of it. You're really well proportioned. You have a beautiful face, too," says Wai Lan.

"No. My breasts are my best feature. Everyone tells me."

As Ga Ling slides under the water, Wai Lan marvels at her tolerance for the heat. Ga Ling rests there, eyes and mouth pressed into a calm smile, her arms folded serenely over her chest. *Ha,* thinks Wai Lan. *You're too trusting.* As she considers tickling Ga Ling out of her complacency, contemplating whether to go for her ribs or her throat, she is struck by the sight of her friend's naked body under the bright water. It looks so puffy and lifeless, unnaturally pale except for the tiny green veins trickling over it like weeds. Seeing her like this makes Wai Lan remember that they are already seventeen, alive but growing older with every moment. "We need something better," she whispers.

In their time together, he had felt such a strange combination of ease and anticipation: a desire to know her and an eagerness to reveal himself to her. And he'd felt something of this from her, too, even if there were moments when she seemed to turn parts of herself away from him. Perhaps she regretted telling him her secrets—though he's sure she kept many more to herself. Perhaps she'd been on some kind of quest, and he'd merely been some kind of a distraction. *Well, at least I've been that for her*, he thinks.

They first get the idea for the parties from the boy Ga Ling starts dating. He picks her up Saturday afternoon and is there the next morning eating pork buns straight from the steamer with his shirt off while Ga Ling makes tea. He is tanned, scrawny, and tight-limbed, with a childish face. His name is Kit. On his third Sunday at the apartment, he asks Wai Lan why she doesn't ever go to the clubs with them. Wai Lan tells him she's better off staying home with a book. Ga Ling laughs. Wai Lan says she isn't a gambler because she isn't stupid. Even if men bought her drinks all night and she got in for free, she isn't about to risk an entire shift's pay on the tables.

"Sounds like you could use a little extra income," says Kit.

"Hey—" Ga Ling pinches his arm. "I said I'd ask her myself."

"What?" says Wai Lan.

Kit explains about throwing a get-together.

"People do them all the time, all kinds of people," he assures her. "I already told Ga Ling that I'll run it for you ladies if you split the profits fifty-fifty."

Wai Lan, thinking she has nothing to lose, agrees.

For the party they take the furniture from the front room up to the roof and cover it with tarp. They move Ga Ling's cot out of her side of the bedroom and into Wai Lan's so that Kit can run a poker and dice game out of it. They buy rice wine by the gallon, which the girls sell for a half mun a glass to the dozen guests crammed into the apartment. They drink and dance to the radio until early morning, when someone in the building complains about the noise and has to be paid off while the guests stumble out drunk. At the end of the night, Kit fans out the hundred mun he's taken on his own, just from the games.

"You're so smart!" says Ga Ling, and Kit laughs as she throws her arms around his neck.

"Let's do it again," says Wai Lan.

They throw another party, then another. Wai Lan learns quickly from Ga Ling, a natural host—flirty, persuasive, and charmingly authoritative. By the third party, they have netted some twenty-odd guests, added gin and whisky to the bar, and hired some of Kit's jazz musician friends to play.

But it's the games that pay them all so well, and they make this their specialty. Ga Ling and Wai Lan, wanting to secure their clientele, go to clubs and make the acquaintance of eager young men with cash in their pockets who sit alone looking as if they'd like a good time but have nobody to have it with. They give the men handwritten cards with information about the party and tell them to drop by the apartment.

They also invite several pretty girls from the factory, teaching the ones who don't already know how to wheedle drinks and food out of the men. If they get the men to spend more than usual, Ga Ling and Wai Lan give them either a small percentage of the proceeds or a gift—a pair of stockings, a vanity case. Most of the time, Wai Lan notices, they don't have to give the girls anything; everyone's out looking for a good time, and when they come to the apartment, they can have it for nothing.

Sing goes up into the mountains. He leaves in the night and keeps walking until sunrise. On some days he comes home with an extraordinary lightness in his body and barely more than a sheen of sweat on his skin. On other days the heat steams through his cotton shirt and soaks his chest. He notices the morning sunlight glancing through the dense crowns of the magnolia trees, and on one occasion feels a moment of panic when he mistakes this brilliance for wildfire as it gleams off a piece of glass. Sometimes the wind teases his skin like a mosquito; at other times it eludes him, the air damp as a sponge. Once in a while, he experiences brief moments when all these sensations melt into something altogether antiseptic and characterless; he'll suddenly feel free and undisturbed, empty of thought and emotion. But as soon as he becomes aware of how free and undisturbed he feels, he'll see a hand in the water or her black hair pooled below her neck. Turning onto a particular path or rushing past a certain home, he'll find himself in a deserted alley or under the tendrils of a banyan tree that he can't remember taking himself to.

Kit eventually moves the gaming room to the kitchen, where he installs a velvet curtain for privacy and a mean-looking ex-con for security. The bedrooms they rent to their guests in thirty-minute slots during the party. Wai Lan expresses some reservations at first, but since Kit and Ga Ling seem to think nothing of it, she lets it go. It brings in extra money after all, though she doesn't like returning to her bedroom at the end of the night and being faced with the leftovers of other people's desire. She pulls on a pair of gloves and collects all the junk into a wastebasket—underwear, wine glasses, cigarette butts. Sometimes she comes across a lost earring or a scarf that she thinks is pretty and might consider keeping it for herself. But she knows that the only occasions she would have to wear such items would be at the parties, where customers are likely to recognize their lost items. And while she knows enough to project confident innocence in the face of accusation, she still can't bring herself to feign ownership of something she has no original claim to. So rather than hoard these items away, she throws them in with the junk and tosses everything in the public bins in front of the building.

After some time, Kit moves in with Ga Ling, who goes part-time at the factory, then quits altogether. By way of explanation, she says that Kit is taking care of her so well that she doesn't need her day job. Wai Lan notices that during the week Kit sometimes brings home a friend and, after they've had a few drinks together, leaves him alone in the bedroom with Ga Ling. She'll hear some grunting and moaning on the other side of the board, a moment of quiet, then a door opening and closing. A day or two later, Ga Ling will be showing off a new dress or hairstyle, or Kit will have an expensive bottle of whisky on the table. For weeks Wai Lan continues to pretend she's ignorant about what is happening. Then one evening Ga Ling comes to her door and tells her an extra friend has come along.

"There's no one to keep him company," she says with a friendly shyness that Wai Lan hasn't seen since their first day together at school. Ga Ling lowers her head and raises her eyes, biting her bottom lip in appeal. "Please," she asks.

It doesn't snow here, so, talk me through it: grey mist on mountains; dirt-cloudy breath; white, mirror lakes; a car window. Rain. Where we used to live. Talk me through it. Words unlock, wooed from their moorings; leave the finite, the solid. Dreams: black streets without temperature and my fingertip pressed against the sky, tracing circles, looking for evidence of travelers.

It's the last day of factory work for Wai Lan. Even after giving Kit his share, she can still earn a day's pay or more in half an hour. In the beginning, she finds many of her customers repulsive, some of them sad. To get away from their faces and the stink of their sweat and mouths, she often finds her thoughts turning to Sing. She wishes that she could have been at once older and more pure for him. She shakes out such thoughts with each untying of her hair and tries not to remember.

Months go by. Wai Lan does not spend any of her earnings on dresses or hats like Ga Ling does. Instead, she stuffs the folded notes in a cookie tin that she keeps under a wood panel in the floor. Each time, after she returns the tin to its secret place, she stands in front of the washbowl and rinses herself off. She keeps telling herself that she has to save, save for something more important ahead, that she needs this to get to the life that is meant for her. She doesn't know what that life is yet, but she knows it has to be more than what she sees in her mother or in poor Ga Ling, whom she's grown to pity. One day she looks at her friend and realizes how much she's changed. Her soft, lovely face has become hard and worn; her eyes have lost their bright mischief and are permanently glazed from booze and drugs. When Wai Lan asks her one evening what she wants to do with her life, Ga Ling replies, "You think too much, Wai Lan. Enjoy life now, while it's good."

One day Wai Lan receives an offer from a client. He's a businessman from Shanghai who has recently bought a club and is looking for new girls. He makes it sound decent—better money and protection, but not *so* good, she thinks, that she can't refuse. That the offer comes at a time when she doesn't consider herself desperate, when she can feel her own importance in having a choice and making a decision, makes the offer seem even more appealing.

In the end she can't think of a way to tell Ga Ling and Kit about it. One evening she simply puts together a small case of her things. On her way out, she lets her hand fall from the doorknob and sets the case down next to the front door, turning back to the kitchen to tell them she is going out for a bit.

"Get me some smokes from the store," says Kit, drunk and mildly irritated by Ga Ling's arms, which are draped over his shoulders like a heavy scarf he can't be bothered to remove.

"We need bread, too," says Ga Ling.

"Okay," says Wai Lan. She heads out into the softly raining night with her suitcase, walking quickly in the opposite direction from the store. In her stealthy briskness she feels like a criminal, each step pushing away the burden of survival so that by the time she reaches the bus stop, she is glad to be emptied of everything but the anticipation of headlights streaking through the darkness. Years later, when she feels older and done with wanting, she might think back to this evening and remember the hard, unfriendly ground through her soles, the hopeful catch of air in her lungs as she counted her bus fare in her damp palm. And the small sting of sorrow she felt at the sight of the girl and the boy—how they looked to be melting into each other like candles under the bright kitchen light.

VII.

A feast has been laid out, the fires lit. The whole village has been invited. Over the years, stories had floated back of Yip Wai Lan's latest scandals and misadventures. Tables of women marvel, suspicious: *What does she want? She had nowhere else to go.* Tables of men marvel, wary: *Can you believe, she still wanted him. Can you believe, he still wanted her.*

They were glad she'd left; they missed her, too.

In the years before Wai Lan's return, Sing has been jealous. Of each object she has touched, each person she has passed, each person who has looked at her or not (though how could they not look at her), each word she has spoken that he has not heard.

Now inside the room, they can still hear the clanging celebration of the village, though they hardly notice it. Much as they do not notice the baying dogs, or the faint roar of the river, or the moon and its slow, striking clouds.

She sits next to the bureau. (The ink well is dry; the sheafs of paper rest in the drawer.)

Her palms balance in her red, beaded lap.

He thinks she looks strange: innocently stiff. She seems weighted down by the shiny, padded fabric. Though he has been wanting it for all these years, he is on the verge of forgetting that slender stroke of body underneath. He unhooks the button on his ceremonial collar, then moves her toward the bed by the shoulders as if she were a sleepy child. They sit on the edge of the bed. The oil lamp flickers a little, dies.

"Wai Lan, there is so much to get through," he says.

"Let me do it," she replies. Her voice is surprisingly large in the dark. She tugs open buttons and knots with bored familiarity.

She takes his hand and pulls it inside the fabric, resting it on her waist. His hand is cold, but she doesn't flinch.

It horrifies him then, the thought of her knowing her hold over him. He thought he cared about honor and reputation, but he would commit any sin if she asked him to. His regret has robbed and diminished him. He wants her to know. He wants to leave it in the past. He wants no desire.

She never presumed that he still wanted her. She just knew that he did. She is embarrassed and saddened by this knowledge, trying to hide it, trying to hide how careful she is being so as not to let him feel too clearly in charge, too owed, knowing he will see through this as an act of condescension. She is trying not to ignore her power over him—how she wounded him in the past, how he wounded her, how the difference was that she intended to do so, thinking it was for everyone's good. It is all a difficult balance; it's all she thinks about. Her effort is a continuous, ugly monument.

He finds her too obedient...too compliant...too reasonable. Yes, she is too reasonable. She didn't come back hurt or defiant or humbled. She wasn't fearful of rejection. She didn't behave like someone who doubted her worth.

With each movement he feels as if he is wading against an angry swell, further and further out to sea.

He wants this, he must. This is as far as she can see.

He is gentle, but not so gentle that it qualifies suspicion. He is not unsure; he is biding his time.

She came back. And married him under an almost full moon on a summer evening. Drunken strings of lights shine through the trees and over the tops of walls, red firecracker paper scattered on the ground. Men and women drink, talking about the couple in a general manner. Carcasses litter the tables. Foam clings to the sides of half-drained glasses. She came back.

Night after night they sleep, but rarely at the same time. Without knowing it, they take turns watching each other. Sometimes they lay their head near the other's chest and listen for the heartbeat: steady, secret, out of reach.

BAD INFLUENCE

AFTER LUNCH, MAYLING CHAN reminded her assistant that she would be leaving the office early to meet her brother, who was coming into San Diego on the four o'clock bus. She felt the need to mention this again at two, and once more at three, like a nervous tic that had suddenly manifested. Mayling hadn't seen her brother in almost six years, and his imminent return provoked an unfamiliar anxiety in her, like a lottery winner afraid of losing her ticket. In Mayling's case, she found herself doubting her ability to hold onto that small, crucial piece of information—*Nelson. July 15th. Four o'clock.* Any distraction and it would slip from her memory, or she'd mix up the time, or she might not recognize her brother when she saw him (although how much, she wondered, could a person change?).

She planned her route so that she'd get to the Greyhound terminal a quarter of an hour early, but as it turned out, the I-5 was congested—a motorcycle accident—and she ended up arriving twenty minutes late and a little flustered. Almost to her disappointment, she spotted her brother straight away: he was sitting on a bench next to the vending machine, scruffy with a duffle bag between his feet and a beat-up looking camera around his neck.

"Nelson?"

"Hey, Mayling!" Her brother jumped up and threw his arms around her in a bony embrace, smelling faintly of wood smoke and industrial soap.

"You must be tired," said Mayling. "Let's get you home."

Nelson stood in place, smiling nervously as if waiting for a punchline. When Mayling clarified, "My place," Nelson swung the duffle over his shoulder and started walking to the car.

During the drive, Nelson tuned the radio to a Mexican music station at a volume that was too loud for conversation and kept his eyes fixed on the view outside his window, holding his camera up to his face every so often. Mayling wondered about his interest in the landscape, which seemed to her unremarkable—the grey, yawning freeway flanked by parched hills, steel towers, and clusters of hastily made houses. It didn't occur to her at the time that her lack of regard for it might have stemmed from the same cause as Nelson's interest: it was where they had both grown up. In any case, Nelson's preoccupation gave Mayling frequent opportunities to steal glances at him. She found herself looking for signs of change rather than familiarity.

Nelson's hair now reached his shoulders in wild, thick waves.

His cheekbones had sharpened, and his skin was several shades darker—the kind of leathery, rawboned tan that came from working or sleeping outdoors. He was, however, still handsome enough to stir some light envy in Mayling. When they would visit relatives in Hong Kong, their parents would often joke, "Mayling got the meat and potatoes. Nelson got the gravy," meaning that Mayling had brains and common sense while her brother had the looks and charm. But he had more than that. Mayling used to think of him as a magician, able to alchemize the sad, angry air around the dinner table into embarrassed smiles or eruptions of unexpected laughter in a way that she never could. She knew she didn't have the imagination or the courage for it. When they were children, Mayling, three years older, was regularly tasked with tracking down her brother, who had a habit of tottering off in department stores with gaggles of cooing teenage girls. Come dinner time, he was often nowhere to be found. No amount of scolding or explaining could convince Nelson that it wasn't all a game of hide-and-seek to which Mayling was a willing accomplice. Once she spent almost an hour searching the neighborhood before finding him napping in a neighbor's tree house. Mayling had slung Nelson over her back like a sack of coal and carried him home, not minding too much his small fist pulling the neck of her t-shirt out of shape or the cold, spreading drool patch on her shoulder.

They were not that close as they grew older. Mayling excelled academically and eventually earned a scholarship to law school. Nelson sailed through high school with a freewheeling, kamikaze agility, delighting in finding common ground with the most fearsome jocks, the most misunderstood loners, and almost everyone else in between. Nelson had been voted class president without having actually run two years in a row; on both occasions, he graciously declined. He finished senior year with his own fan club, a group of besotted sophomore girls who called themselves "the Chanatics" and left pot cookies, love letters, and underwear in his locker. He took the cookies and left the underwear and the letters.

After graduation, Nelson told his parents that he'd decided to put off college to go traveling for a year. "Kids do it all the time in Europe," he assured them, as if Europe were just a couple of towns over. "It's called a gap year." He embraced them when he left, promising he'd be okay. At first, when relatives and neighbors used to ask about him, their parents would mournfully tell of postcards sent every few months—from Alaska, Montreal, Greenland, for Pete's sake. *This is a good place. Don't worry about me,* he'd write. But they did worry. That he'd get hurt working on a trawler or chopping trees or fall in with a bad crowd and forget he was loved, needed. Year two, a postcard came from Peru. Year three, nothing.

During those first few years, Mayling contacted everyone from high school she could think of, looking for Nelson spottings. She checked online message boards in English, Chinese, and Spanish. But whatever leads came up she kept to herself, not wanting to get their parents' hopes up. More often than not, they led nowhere. Eventually she decided it was out of her hands. Her brother, for whatever reason, didn't want to be found, and there was nothing else to do but continue reassuring her parents that their son was fine, just fine. After some time, they knew to stop asking, eventually submitting to a kind of bright, fragile stoicism sometimes associated with the prematurely bereaved.

Then one morning in July Mayling got the call. Nelson announced that he was passing through San Diego in a few days en route to Mexico, and could she put him up for a night. Mayling thought fleetingly of that phone call as she drove, and of the dulled astonishment she'd felt—not so much that her brother had called, but that he hadn't sounded like a stranger.

"Take this exit, would you?" said Nelson, turning down the radio. When they got off the ramp, he stuffed the camera into his duffle bag and pointed to a Chinese restaurant up ahead.

"At five o'clock?" said Mayling.

"I'm starving," Nelson pleaded, "and I've really missed this shit."

As the young, ponytailed waitress showed them to a booth, Nelson whispered something to her that provoked a bashful giggle from the girl. He ordered for the both of them—fried noodles, a whole roast duck, and garlic bak choy—in Cantonese that was so halting it made Mayling wince. She thought briefly of Saturday mornings at Chinese School, taking vocabulary tests and reciting poems while Nelson snuck off to the skate park or the video arcade. Still, she saw it as an opportunity to warm him up to talking about himself.

"Glad to see you've kept up the Chinese," said Mayling "I suppose you can say 'roast duck' in ten different languages now."

Nelson smiled faintly as he poured tea into two small cups: first Mayling's, then his own. Mayling watched him concentrate his gaze on the cup of tea between his hands, bringing it to his lips at measured intervals and letting loose deep, satisfied sighs after each sip. Mayling started to grow restless. She took out her phone to check her messages, prompting Nelson to finally speak.

"Did you, uh, keep your word?"

"About Mom and Dad?" Mayling nodded. She put the phone back down on the table. "You put me in an awkward position."

"It would upset them to know I was here."

"So you said." Mayling took a sip of tea. Too weak. "This needs to brew longer," she said. "So. Have you been okay?"

Nelson shrugged. "Life's pretty simple these days—work, eat, sleep. The only expectations people have of me are 'don't be late,' and 'don't break anything, asshole.' Suits me fine."

"Emphasis on 'asshole,'" said Mayling. The words surprised her, and she braced herself for Nelson to fire back an insult or make some kind of dramatic exit. But the comment didn't even break his smile; rather, it fixed it in place, the look in his eyes hovering between amusement and provocation.

"Well, I guess we agree on something," he said, sounding almost conciliatory. Then, brightly, "So, Sis, tell me about your life. Then it's my turn. Deal?"

Mayling felt the wind go out of her sails, though she couldn't think what it was she'd been readying herself for. She found herself dutifully describing her job as a patent lawyer, employing the same spiel she used at bars and parties, where she'd insist on the general dullness of her work, then throw out a few entertaining examples of wild inventions or dramatic copyright battles.

Nelson asked if she was happy with her life, and Mayling said she couldn't complain. She had risen quickly at her firm, which, if not the most prestigious, was a respectable stepping stone to other prospects. She'd bought a house earlier that year without help from her parents (many of her peers couldn't say the same), and she had a circle of close friends whom she saw on a regular basis. She was not yet thirty, and she had all of this. Yes, things were going quite well.

Nelson had been listening closely and with great investment. Finally he said, "Sounds to me like you deserve every good thing that's happened to you." He raised his cup. "I always knew you'd do good." He spoke with a nostalgic sort of pride that Mayling found surprising and a little sad.

"Anyone special in your life?" he asked.

Mayling shook her head.

"No lucky guy or girl?"

"I was seeing someone for a while. But between our crazy work schedules—she was a medical resident—we barely got to see each other. It just got to the point—"

"Don't work so hard, Sis. You deserve happiness as much as the next person. Just remember that."

When the food arrived, Nelson tore into it as if he hadn't seen a hot meal in days. It brought out his talkative streak, and he spoke through mouthfuls of food about a connection he had in Mexico, some guy who was building a solar-powered school. He was going down to work with the guy for a few months, then see what else came up. It seemed he had become something of an expert in ecologically sustainable construction, and was able to speak on the subject with casual authority. But not for long. He got distracted easily, jumping from one anecdote to another—studying with a shaman in Peru, building a film set for a Hollywood director in the Amazon rainforest, watching a crew member on a fishing trawler fall overboard into the treacherous Bering Sea. Mayling worked hard to keep track of all the people and places floating in and out of Nelson's world, trying to make sense of the timeline. Was it Peru and Brazil, then Greenland? Or the other way around? At one point, she guiltily caught her attention wandering to something ambiguous her boss had said that morning, and at another point, to the man she'd met during a work trip in London and had been meaning to call. Eventually, Nelson threw down his chopsticks, emitted a long, satisfied belch, and slumped back in his seat.

"I think I overdid it," he grinned, patting his stomach.

"Moron," said Mayling, shaking her head at the amount of food still on the table.

They decided to box up the remainder of the roast duck and grab a drink before heading home. Mayling drove them to an Irish bar near her house in Ocean Beach. It was not her regular spot, but she'd chosen it to minimize the risk of bumping into someone they knew and having word somehow travel back to their parents. Mayling did a quick scan of the place, which was filling up with the happy hour crowd, before deciding it was safe for them to stay. She threw back two IPAs with a double shot of Knob Creek; Nelson followed suit.

By the second round, they had hit it off with a couple at the pool table, who invited them for a game. The Chans won easily, drank their winnings, and opened up the next game. Two loud, cheerful advertising executives stepped in. They proved to be decent players. Mayling valiantly held her game, but Nelson didn't take his drink well and was getting sloppy. They took their defeat in good humor, and Mayling bought herself and the victors a round of drinks, while Nelson leaned into the bar with his head in his hands.

"Bad influence, you," he groaned.

"Feather-ass lightweight, you," said Mayling. "Let's get you some air."

It was chillier on the beach than they'd expected, but it had the desired effect, stinging Nelson into alertness and quickening his movements. Soon he was skipping and jumping along the water's edge in an effort to keep warm. In the bluish, half-moon glow, against the crashing waves, he resembled some feral creature performing a nocturnal mating dance.

"Over there!" said Nelson, marching towards a bonfire in the distance. "I need to get warm."

The small group that was congregated around the fire looked to Mayling like a collection of dreadlocks and homemade sweaters. Everyone was talking and laughing as one of them strummed a guitar, and a glass pipe about the size of a baby's arm was slowly making its way around the circle. Nelson asked them for a hit. He held up the takeout bag. "Trade you for some duck?"

It turned out that no one in the group ate meat, but they were a friendly bunch. Someone pulled out beers from a cooler and invited Nelson and Mayling to join them. Mayling passed on the pipe, but collected both the beers and sat down in an awkward cross-legged position. Nelson had found a place on the other side of the circle and was deep in conversation with a bearded man who was drumming on a pair of bongos without much commitment.

Guess we'll be here a while, thought Mayling.

She drank one beer. She drank the other beer. Then she stuck the empty cans in the sand and started pushing cold handfuls of sand around them until they were almost covered, resulting in a knobby mound with two holes peeping out at the top. She drew a smiley mouth underneath with her finger and said to it, "What are *you* smiling at?"

She understood that she'd drunk more than she'd planned to, and that she probably shouldn't drive home. They'd walk the ten, fifteen blocks, whatever it was. Whenever it was time. Which was not yet. No, she wasn't ready yet. She edged herself closer to the fire and held up her palms, drawing in the warmth and closing her eyes so that she could feel it on her eyelids and maybe rest a while. She let the roar of the ocean close in around her like a blanket. When it had numbed the voices and the music and the crackling of the fire to a dampened drone, it was finally quiet enough for her to remember that she'd prepared a whole damned speech for Nelson on the way to the Greyhound terminal. She had meant to bring up their father's heart attack that spring, their mother's paranoia after their neighbors' house had been burgled while they were sleeping, how her mother had gone so far as to demand a gun for protection, insisting she never felt safe here the way she did in Hong Kong. Mayling had selected some choice words about all these things. But they were not what she hated her brother for.

She hated how her parents had been reduced to a pathetic, funereal longing, how their mantelpiece was still decorated with Nelson's pictures, though they could hardly bring themselves to talk about him. How every Christmas her father still cooked more than the three of them could manage, and afterwards her mother would wait until Mayling had finished putting her shoes on in the hall, handing her a carefully packed box of leftovers and standing in the doorway as she walked down the drive to her car. She had no idea how long their mother would stand there, staring into the distance with one hand in the air, but catching sight of her in the rearview mirror, she knew her mother was hoping for some sign—an unusual noise or movement disturbing the quiet of their street—that meant that this year, Nelson had decided to come back and surprise them.

Nelson would know none of these things, would never know anything beyond a vague, romantic notion of the true extent of the wounds he had made. And in that moment, enveloped in the roar of the ocean, Mayling decided that it was wrong to tell him. He hadn't earned it.

When she opened her eyes again, she saw her brother playing guitar to a rapt audience and trying to sing something that sounded like "Tangled Up in Blue" with a duck leg hanging from his mouth, stopping every so often to take a bite out of it. He winked at Mayling, who returned a nod.

Yes. Nelson would never think of anyone but Nelson. He would never say sorry. He would never thank Mayling for staying. Mayling couldn't find the anger she was looking for— only a weird, pressed-down hollowness. Perhaps if Mayling had been less dutiful, less indulgent towards her brother, things would have turned out differently. Perhaps they'd be exactly the same, and Nelson would have remained beyond the grasp of anyone foolish enough to love him.

"Are you sure you don't want any?" A smiling girl with blonde dreadlocks presented the pipe to Mayling as if it were a graduation scroll.

"No, thank you," said Mayling. "I don't really smoke."

"Positive?" she said. "Last chance."

Mayling noticed an incongruity between the girl's appearance and her manner, which possessed a certain polish. As the girl waited for Mayling's response, still smiling, still offering, it came to her. She was courteous in that earnest, practiced way that Mayling recognized as particular to children who have endured years of parental fussing and coaching. She couldn't have been more than eighteen or so, and her prettiness was of the clean, wholesome variety. Mayling had dated girls with a similar quality, but this one's earnestness gave her an air of childish vulnerability that sparked her sympathy. She saw a young girl in a neat suburban living room, wearing her best Sunday dress and carefully balancing a tray of hors d'oeuvres at one of her parents' social functions, diligently working her way around the guests and being ignored, or patted on the head, or, as she got older, touched a second too long in the small of her back.

"Do you speak to your parents?" she blurted out.

"What?" The girl held onto her smile, pretending not to have heard her.

Mayling smiled, too, and shook her head, pretending she hadn't asked. She took the pipe from the girl.

"What the hell," she said. "I'm celebrating."

She held the pipe above her head and shouted over her brother's song, "To my brother, Nelson! Here for one night only, ladies and gentlemen. I shall miss you."

Nelson took the duck leg out of his mouth, saluted Mayling with it, and resumed the song. In that moment, and for years afterwards, Mayling appreciated that Nelson didn't attempt any further response, didn't say, "There's no need to miss me, I'll be back before you know it." In fact, he didn't say anything that suggested they would ever see each other again—not that night, when they stumbled back to Mayling's house through the dimly lit streets, or the next morning, as he ran out to the car honking in the drive, explaining that it was his ride across the border.

THE WOMAN IN THE CLOSET

AUGUST

IN THE SPACE OF a few hours, Granny Ng was made an official member of the village and given her own blue tent, just like the others had. Over a hundred tents dotted the southeastern side of Hong Kong Park like giant petals from outer space. That's how they'd once seemed to her back in the days when she still lived with her son and daughter-in-law. Back then, she would take her morning stroll around the turtle pond with Maru, her daughter-in-law's shi'itsu. She'd occasionally look over to that strange blue sight, and whenever she saw people moving among the tents, she would turn away, embarrassed for staring. She had never given much thought to why people lived that way. Then one morning, a middle-aged woman with a sleek black bob and a pink tracksuit stopped her at the turtle pond. The woman said she'd noticed her walking her dog there in the mornings, and asked if she was all right. She had her hand on Granny Ng's arm and a concerned, hopeful look on her face. Granny Ng had to admit that she was feeling hungry, having only had a few crackers for breakfast. The woman—she introduced herself as Kitty —seemed well-spoken and polite, so Granny Ng was surprised when, after answering a few questions about her home life, her new acquaintance led her toward the mass of blue tents. They stopped at an awning at the southern perimeter of the tents where a short, silver-bearded man was stirring a pot of soup on a camp stove.

"Uncle Chow, this is Granny Ng," said Kitty. "Her son and daughter-in-law want to kick her out of her apartment and put her in an old people's home at the end of the month. She doesn't want to go."

Granny felt her cheeks warm with embarrassment. The silver-bearded man tasted a spoonful of the soup and nodded slowly, though it wasn't clear if it was to himself or to Kitty. He turned abruptly, wiped his hands on the front of his overalls, and invited Granny Ng to sit on one of the plastic children's stools dotted around the outdoor kitchen.

"Granny, take the weight off your feet. Ah Kitty, give her some of this soup, will you?" He brought over another stool and sat facing her. "Well, Granny, I'm sorry to hear your son doesn't want to take care of you. This kind of thing is getting more and more common these days."

Granny Ng blinked at the bowl of beef soup in her hands and nodded.

"But the fact is that you still have somewhere to stay, true? None of the people here can say the same."

Kitty looked concerned. "Tell him, Granny Ng. Tell Uncle Chow what you told me."

The soup smelled so good to Granny Ng. She hadn't had beef soup in years; her son and daughter-in-law were converts to Taoism, and had taken a three-year vow of vegetarianism. She brought the bowl to her lips, then hesitated. It was too hot to drink right then, but she didn't want to be rude. Then again, she'd already burnt her tongue several times that week to avoid her daughter-in-law hitting her for eating too slowly. She peered around hopefully for a spoon.

"Granny, please allow me to speak for you," said Kitty. She squatted on the ground next to Granny Ng and looked imploringly at the silver-bearded man. "It's terrible in there, Uncle Chow. The staff beat the old people and steal their valuables. They hide their letters and have to be bribed in order to hand them over. On visiting days, they put on a big show of caring for the residents so the children don't get concerned, but as soon as they leave it all starts again. We can't let this poor granny end up in a place like that, can we? We can't let her go from bad to worse."

Uncle Chow scratched his beard. "Which old people's home is this?"

"Does it matter?" sighed Kitty. Then she lowered her head as if admitting defeat. "My mother was in that kind of home."

Uncle Chow considered Granny Ng as she blew on her soup. "How are you, Granny? Are you enjoying the soup?"

"It's delicious," she said, blowing harder on the soup. It was still too hot to taste. "The best I've ever had."

"Uncle Chow here used to be a cook," said Kitty. "He worked for some of the best hotels in the city."

"Oh? How did you end up here?" asked Granny Ng.

When Uncle Chow smiled, she could see how densely packed his teeth were, like a dolphin's. She imagined him pulling out one of his silver whiskers and flossing with it.

"Luck," he replied.

"Luck?" said Granny Ng. "You think you're lucky?"

"I didn't say what kind of luck, Granny. Drink up your soup. It should be cool enough now."

Uncle Chow and Kitty pitched a tent for Granny Ng close to the center of the settlement. Although it wasn't something she usually did, Kitty accompanied Granny Ng to the small apartment she shared with her son and daughter-in-law and helped her gather some belongings into a duffle bag. It was clear that Granny Ng hadn't packed a bag in some time; Kitty had to keep telling her to put things back, or explain that some things, like the rice cooker and the ironing board, were not practical to bring. Before they left, Granny Ng wrote a note for her son and taped it to the refrigerator door:

> Dear Son,
> I have received a call from a relative who is very sick, and I must visit her at once. I don't know how long I'll be gone. Please don't worry about me. I'll be in touch.
> Please take care of yourself,
> Your mother

Don't call the police, Son, she thought, *And don't worry about me.* Once things were more settled, she would write again. She thought he wouldn't approve of her making her own arrangements in this way, and might even feel as if he'd let her down. But she felt it was the right decision; in the long run, her daughter-in-law would be happier, which meant that her son had a chance of being happier.

That first week, Kitty was a constant presence, bringing with her visitors such as Brother Shek, a construction worker. He lined Granny Ng's tent with mesh sheets that he assured her would protect her from bugs and damp. Brother Shek's wife gave her acupressure massages for her aching back, while a young woman called Miss Kwan came by to donate a pair of gloves.

Uncle Chow explained how the village worked: the timetable for communal meals, the mail system, the procedures for submitting suggestions and complaints and so on. Meanwhile, Kitty showed her where to go for drinking water and washing facilities. Her favorite spots were the public bathrooms near the British Council, which tended to be the cleanest, but she warned her not to go there after dark. She showed her spots around town where she could collect cans and bottles for recycling, the best underpasses from which to hawk goods without being bothered by police, and the best flyovers from which to beg—or as they liked to call it, "ask for donations."

At first, Granny Ng did not sleep well in her new environment. She didn't mind the ground, which was not much harder than her previous bed, or the smallness of the space, though it would have been nice to be able to stand up instead of crawling and stooping all the time. What bothered her were the noises, which seemed to go on all night through to the morning: fellow tent dwellers chatting and cooking, voices and songs from their radios, teenagers' yells and screams floating over from the other side of the park. Traffic never seemed to stop, either, the roar of engines and horns constant through the night; she wondered where these people were driving to under the cover of darkness, and when they planned to catch up on the sleep they were losing. She found she was stiffer than usual. In the mornings, it took about half an hour of stretching and walking about before she felt normal again.

Granny Ng learned that people had come to the tent village for different reasons. Some had lost their homes during the last financial crisis. Many of the men in their late forties and fifties were construction workers who'd been laid off and couldn't find steady work.

Miss Kwan was one of the newer residents. She'd lost her sales job at a securities firm three months before, though she'd been able to keep the news from her parents, who had emigrated to Canada several years prior. For the past three months, on the last Thursday of each month, Miss Kwan would put on her old work suit and walk over to the other side of the park for a standing lunch date with an old classmate. Her friend, who managed a cosmetics store, would be waiting on a bench by the koi pond. She and her friend took turns treating each other. Miss Kwan had to save for three weeks in order to buy two rice box lunches from their favorite restaurant. She'd never finish her meal, claiming she was full, or that she was trying to lose weight, but the truth was that she was keeping half of her lunch box for her evening meal. Afterwards, she would return to her tent, slip her work suit into its plastic cover, and put it carefully away until the next time.

Granny Ng got the scoop on her neighbors from Kitty, who happily volunteered details of their life stories, though she would get vague when it came to Uncle Chow.

"He lost his job at a hotel, a good one I think, but no one really knows the details. He makes a bit here and there nowadays by repairing electrical items—radios, lamps, clocks, that kind of thing. We're not even sure how long he's been here. Find the oldest, longest-standing resident and they'll tell you Uncle Chow was already here and running things when they arrived."

Granny Ng found it odd that Kitty knew so little about her friend. Then again, despite several weeks of confidences, Kitty had yet to tell Granny Ng her own story of coming to live in the tent village. She'd once mentioned a husband, but Granny Ng sensed her reluctance to elaborate. And while she tried to ignore the casual gossip from some of her fellow villagers—the husband was a drinker, a gambler, a wife-beater—she couldn't help but invest in a version of Kitty's past, one filled with adversity, suffering, and courage. This led to a newfound appreciation of her friend's cheerful efficiency and eagerness to help, which at first, she had to admit, she had rather taken for granted and at times even found a little intrusive. Whatever the case, it seemed to Granny Ng that Kitty was content there, and this inspired in her the possibility that she could be, too.

Despite her circumstances, Granny Ng was quite good at keeping herself clean and presentable. She bathed and did laundry in public washrooms, and even looked respectable enough to occasionally pass through shining hotel lobbies and use their bathrooms. She was careful to avoid going to the same hotels too often and to bring only one or two garments at a time to wash. Once, noticing the suspicious gaze of the bathroom attendant, she said she'd spilled something on herself in the restaurant and wanted to get the stain out. But maintaining a neat appearance wasn't always helpful: people found it difficult to believe that the well-kempt old woman sitting on the pedestrian flyover really needed to beg. Some of them would say, "Come on Granny, you've had your fun. Now, stop slumming it and go home to your family. They'll be worried about you." She'd always ignore the comments and continue to hold out her bowl, feeling it was less shameful to beg from strangers than from family.

OCTOBER

Granny Ng had been living in the tent village for forty-two days when the city officials removed her and about twenty other newcomers from the park. When Uncle Chow asked them why, the officials told him they'd been given orders to prevent the spreading of the tent village. Granny Ng assumed there must be some kind of understanding with the old-timer tent dwellers, since they were left alone. As the officials stood over Granny Ng, watching Brother Shek help her pack up her tent and belongings, they seemed genuinely sorry, even a little embarrassed. Kitty and Uncle Chow gave her small packets and tins of food as well as suggestions about where she could try setting up next. Kitty looked as if she might cry. "I'm so sorry you can't stay, Granny Ng. I feel like I've let you down." Granny Ng patted her on the shoulder and continued packing up her tent. She folded it slowly and with care. *It may just be a sheet of cloth held up by poles*, she thought, *but even a millimeter of fabric can provide a small feeling of security*.

Granny Ng took Kitty's suggestion and tried another tent village in a park about ten miles west. Kitty had taken her to the bus station and pointed to the name of the stop where she had to get off, making her repeat the name three times. She saw her off with a cube of green bean cake wrapped in wax paper and a flask of hot tea.

This new tent village was much smaller, with only perhaps ten or twelve tents. They called themselves an association, and everything was shared. There was no chief, but one of the residents who seemed to speak the most was a gaunt, wiry man called Mr. To. He explained to Granny Ng that as long as she paid 100 HKD a month, she could share their rice, cooking gas, and water. The association had also managed to get some farm land donated to them by a homeless coalition group.

"We started growing vegetables on it about a year a go," said Mr. To. "The land had previously been used for growing pomegranates. It took us months to clear the roots by hand."

"I can help," said Granny Ng. "I know a little about gardening."

"Ah no, Granny," said Mr. To. "It's too much for you. The men have to cycle for almost an hour to get there. Besides, the first crops have just been harvested. We'll sell the vegetables in the park in the next few days. I think we'll make about 1,000 HKD."

Granny Ng nodded.

"You're probably better off collecting recyclables or asking for donations," said Mr. To.

Granny Ng said, "I understand," but really she envied the men. How satisfying it must be to make something that could be sold to appreciative customers. If she couldn't help the association with farming, she could perhaps do other things. She had always been good with her hands, and as a young girl had assisted her father in his studio. He had been a carpenter by trade, but he also made beautiful woodcarvings that he sold to a small number of clients.

She loved to watch him work. During her final year of primary school, she carved a set of six animals, each the size of a child's fist. When, after a week, it became clear that they would little resemble their real life counterparts, she decided to turn them into mythical creatures of her own device. The pig, for example, would have the stripes of a tiger. The bird, whose legs were too thick, would have horse legs. She worked on the carvings every day after school for almost two months. The most difficult one to get right was a creature with the body of a leopard and the head of an elephant; this alone took two weeks. She finally presented the set to her father on his birthday, whose chuckling delight she remembered more clearly than any words of praise he may have uttered. Several days later, when he saw her sorting through blocks of wood for another project, he said, "Daughter, your high school entrance exams are just two months away. I think you should spend your time studying." Granny Ng couldn't recall anything she had made since then. Still, throughout her life, she would occasionally wonder if, had she not become a wife and mother, or if she'd been born in a different time, she might have followed in her father's footsteps.

She went around the park collecting branches and nubs of wood. Then she borrowed a selection of tools from the communal kitchen and workshop—a saw, a cutting knife, several chisels—and set to work. She worked with great concentration, determined to conjure from these coarse pieces of wood a delicately contoured animal. She spent almost an entire day on the project, and by dusk, when she had to return the tools, she was disappointed to have achieved only a crudely shaped figure. Her fellow villagers showed little surprise. A few managed to say, "Good effort, Granny," before retiring to their tents. Disheartened, Granny Ng joined some of the others the next day in collecting cans and bottles for recycling.

DECEMBER

Granny Ng managed to stay in the village for a month before city officials came and cleared out the newcomers. She went to another park, where she stayed for twenty-six days before being moved again. She began worrying about the cooler weather that was coming. Upon leaving the last tent village, she'd been given the name of another park up in the New Territories. A few minutes into the bus ride, Granny Ng fell into a light sleep. When she awoke, she was alarmed to find herself traveling along an open highway, fields and hills sparsely dotted with low-rise houses on either side. At the next stop, she went up to the driver and showed him the piece of paper with the name of the park she was trying to reach written on it.

"Don't worry, Granny," said the driver. "You've still got about six more stops."

"When did we leave Hong Kong Island?"

He shrugged. "About twenty miles back."

Granny Ng returned to her seat. She gazed out of the window at the quiet, unfamiliar landscape—an expanse of sky and dense, green peaks that loomed in the distance. She had not traveled so far from home in years, and those twenty extra miles suddenly felt like another country. Panicked, she pressed the bell and hurried off the bus at the next stop, pausing only to thank the driver. She set down her duffle bag and watched the bus disappear into the pinkish blue horizon.

She realized that she had to get to the other side of the highway. Something told her that whatever she needed was situated there. But even though it seemed relatively quiet, she was afraid to step onto the tarmac in case a vehicle appeared out of nowhere and knocked her flat.

A sudden breeze kicked up, and Granny Ng hugged herself against the chill. She picked up her duffle bag and started walking along the side of the road, squinting at the sunset. After a quarter of an hour, she came to an underpass marked by a sign: *Tin Hau Garden.* An arrow pointed to the other side. It was several degrees cooler in the underpass, which was weakly lit and smelled of damp leaves and urine. She hurried past a peeling mural of children flying kites on a hill and up a sloping path that brought her onto the other side of the highway. Another sign for Tin Hau Garden pointed to a narrow, overgrown path that eventually opened onto a small patch of green. A stone bird fountain stood in the middle, full of mashed leaves and dirty water. Next to it was an iron bench. Granny Ng noticed a memorial plaque on the back of the bench, but she avoided reading it. It made her uncomfortable, this monument after death. She wondered about the person this was dedicated to, how they would feel knowing there was a big, uncomfortable bench in their name. She decided it was useless and in the way—too hard to sit on, let alone sleep on. *Not that I would ever sleep on a bench*, she thought.

Granny Ng decided to set up her sleeping arrangements while there was still some light. A thick line of bushes near the highway seemed a good choice—it provided enough cover from passing cars and people and an escape route of sorts in case she needed one (who knew if unruly teenagers had already claimed this spot for drinking or goodness knows what else). Pulling back some branches and hunching a little, she edged herself in. She beat back some more branches to make enough room to lay down a narrow piece of tarp and unfurled her ground mat and sleeping bag. She then hooked the loops of the tent cover onto overhanging branches. There was just enough room to sit up straight and to lie down. Now that she had made her nest, she felt reluctant to leave it, reassured by the cover it gave. She pulled a flashlight from her duffle bag and laid it down beside her hip. She also pulled out a clock radio and a plastic bag containing a roll of toilet paper, setting them down beside the flashlight. Then she arranged her evening meal: a tangerine, a tin of Spam, and a flask of green tea.

Granny Ng's greatest fear had once been that the older she got, the more likely it would be that she would be forgotten. Her second greatest fear was to be a burden, though that was sometimes the only guarantee of being remembered. Now, munching on the tangerine, she decided it would be ideal to depart from this life without a trace. How nice, she thought, to lie down on a patch of earth and simply be absorbed by rapid degrees throughout the night so that by morning you'd be gone. How efficient. Passersby would not have to deal with the inconvenience of a body, and only delight in finding usefulness in the objects inside the tent: the sleeping bag, the clock radio, the tube of toothpaste, the three sweaters and two pairs of comfortable shoes, the Swiss army knife, the roll of toilet paper, the flashlight, the tin bowl, the pair of metal chopsticks, and the three tins of Spam.

Granny Ng spent the following morning contemplating the house on the other side of the highway. It was low and cream-colored, with a dark glass door. It intrigued her that a family would want to live in the middle of a field with no other houses in sight and a restless, noisy highway right in front. She decided to watch the house and wait for a glimpse of this family. She imagined a young, successful couple ushering their children, a boy and a girl, out of the house each morning and onto the school bus. Perhaps they had a dog. Her daughter-in-law had kept her poor shi'itsu, Maru, cooped up in a cage in the kitchen, and Granny Ng, unable to bear its mournful whining, had taken it upon herself to walk it around the park every morning. *But this family*, she thought, *they have so much space, they could keep a dog of any size and it would be happy.*

Granny Ng watched the house all morning, but no one appeared. She had to get up every half hour or so and walk about to warm herself up and stretch her legs. She had been hungry since waking up, but made herself wait until noon before she ate. She had two and a half tins of Spam left; with rice they could last her a few more days, but on their own she didn't know. She took small bites, washing down the saltiness with sips from her flask of tea, which had now grown tepid and slimy. The food put a weight in her stomach but made her feel colder than before.

She watched the house for the rest of the afternoon; still no one appeared. Eventually, she climbed into her sleeping bag and tried to nap for a while. A horn from a passing truck woke her. She drew back the tent covering and saw a darkening sky streaked with smoky greys and blues. A little while later, at around seven o'clock, she saw a young, small-faced man approach the front door. A salesman? But no; he rummaged in his trouser pocket, fished out a key, and let himself in.

Over the next few days, Granny Ng watched the house and the young man, who emerged each morning in a tie and a short-sleeved shirt, munching on an apple. She watched him for three days. On the fourth, she made her move.

* * *

The gate to the side of the house unlatched lightly, and she stepped into a flat garden with a pear tree at the bottom. She pulled a patio chair under an open window, stood on the chair, and climbed in, slowly lowering herself backwards into the sink. As she brought her left leg towards the floor, she was distracted by her plastic flip-flop sliding off her foot; turning to see it, she lost her balance, caught the edge of the sink for balance, and banged her elbow with a curse.

She leaned back against the sink and took a moment to rub her elbow, then her lower back and thighs. She felt as if she had stones lodged in her joints. As the blood started returning to her limbs, she realized that for the first time in weeks, she didn't feel cold.

The room smelled of warm dust and lemons. Plastic detergent bottles lined a single shelf above a chrome washer dryer. She eyed her distorted reflection in the door: her face stretched like a balloon, her short, greasy hair a smear of black ink. She gathered up her flip-flops and glanced at the wall clock. 8:05 am.

Granny Ng stepped out into a long corridor, her toes nudging the edge of the tatami runner that stretched to the end. In the quiet, her breathing sounded amplified and coarse. She listened for a scrape of a chair, a cough. All she heard was a low hum of electricity. Still, she stood paralyzed with doubt. Maybe she wasn't so original after all. Maybe someone else had got there first.

She considered the closed doors along the corridor, opening the first one on her right. Bathroom. Empty. The next door revealed a thermostat. The opposite door opened onto an office. Next to that was a closet full of towels and bedding. The last door opened onto the master bedroom. No one there. She sighed with relief, then chuckled at her faintheartedness. The end of the corridor revealed an open kitchen on the left and a living room on the right. The kitchen was spacious, with a preparation counter in the middle and shiny orange pots and pans hanging on a metal rafter above it. In the living room there was a large, thin television mounted on the wall and a brown, L-shaped sofa facing it. The sparseness of her surroundings stirred in her feelings of awe and unease. The objects around her seemed to exist within an impersonal kind of order, as if they had been arranged according to an instruction manual. The only suggestion that someone might actually reside there came from the small collection of framed photographs on the living-room side table. Granny Ng picked up a photograph of the young man. He was wearing a graduation cap and gown and had a small, pebble-smooth face with eyes that looked ready to flinch.

"Ah, who's been bullying you, son?" she said softly. He looked like a nice boy, the kind who had good manners. A slight, uncertain smile rested on his pillowy lips. He reminded Granny Ng of the classical poet from the painting, what was its name? In the painting, the poet sat on a rock with cranes perched on branches around him. He was reciting a poem, which was inscribed in the upper right corner of the painting. She had seen the painting throughout her life: as a young girl, she'd seen it in one of her father's art books in his studio; as a student, she'd seen it at the University Museum in Pok Fu Lam; and throughout the rest of her life, she'd encountered the image on t-shirts, mugs, and posters in souvenir shops. But, as with many things now, she couldn't recall its name.

In another photograph, the young man was at a lake, wearing a baggy t-shirt with the letters NYU on it and standing next to an older man with the same pillowy mouth. With one hand, the older man held up a plump, chrome-colored fish the size of a small boy, and with the other hand, he squeezed the young man's shoulder. They were smiling. No, the older man was smiling; the young man seemed to be squinting into the sun or about to cry.

Granny Ng liked the look of the sofa, and thought it couldn't hurt to sit for just a moment. She sank into the cushions and was startled by how soft and comfortable they were. She rubbed her cheek against the cool suede and let out a deep "Aaahhh…"

Then she became aware of a darkly sour odor. She pulled some strands of hair across her face and gingerly sniffed them, then her shirtsleeve. Although she'd tried to keep herself as clean as possible, the salty, earthy smells of the park and her lack of access to a bathroom these last few days had hindered this effort. She suddenly felt filthy, slick with dirt and sweat, and was seized with an urge to scrub herself clean. She went into the bathroom, closed the toilet lid, removed her clothes, and folded them into a neat pile on top.

The shower was glorious. She'd forgotten how good it felt to stand under hot, steaming water. It was so soothing that she almost dozed off. But the jabbing hunger in her stomach jolted her to and made her turn off the water. Squeezing a towel around her, she frowned at the pile of clothes on the toilet seat. She gathered them in her arms and padded across the corridor into the office. This room had a futon sofa, a framed photograph of Mount Fuji, a desk with a computer on it, and a built-in closet with sliding wooden doors. Inside the closet she found some suits and coats hanging in filmy covers. Plastic boxes were stacked in threes, containing t-shirts, sweaters, and jogging pants. The jogging pants she picked out were too long—she had to fold up the ends three times—but the t-shirt fit nicely.

In the kitchen, she found garbage bags under the sink. She pulled one out and started filling it up. First she put in some clothes from the closet: two pairs of thick socks, a sweater, and two t-shirts. Then she went back to the kitchen and collected several tins of Spam, dace in black bean, preserved vegetables, a few packets of ramen noodles, and a liter bottle of mineral water. She wrapped three eggs in a dishcloth. She thought about taking some soap and detergent with which to wash her clothes, then realized she could just come back and use the washer dryer.

Okay, she told herself. *You've got your supplies. Time to go.* But the jabbing in her stomach wouldn't let up. She decided that it couldn't hurt to make herself something to eat. She reasoned, *I've got all day, after all*, and the prospect of hot food was too tempting to pass up. Meanwhile, she might as well throw those dirty clothes into the washer.

Granny Ng cooked some ramen noodles in a saucepan, cracked an egg into it, and ate from a large bowl on the sofa in front of the TV. She was relishing the warmth of the soup too much to pay attention to the bright, flickering images on the screen. She fell asleep with the bowl in her lap and woke later in near-darkness with a shiver, seized by a mild panic, momentarily forgetting where she was and then suddenly feeling cold and heavy with tiredness. In the dark kitchen, the microwave clock glowed at her: 6:45 pm. The young man came home at 7 pm.

Granny Ng grabbed the saucepan and started scrubbing at the noodles that had stuck to the bottom. Then she rinsed off the bowl and the chopsticks, dried everything, and put the items back in their places. She wiped down the counters with a sponge and wiped them again with a paper towel to avoid leaving watermarks.

6:55 pm. The sky was dark outside. The branches of the pear tree at the bottom of the garden had retreated into shadows.

Granny Ng headed to the back of the house towards the laundry room, took the damp clothes out of the washer, and with some effort managed to pull herself onto the sink counter. Then she remembered the garbage bag full of supplies.

"Stupid!" she whispered. She lowered herself back down and hurried into the bedroom. No bag. She went down the hall and searched the office and the kitchen before finally spotting it at the foot of the sofa.

"Friday is good for me, too."

Granny Ng froze at the sound of the young man's voice on the other side of the front door. Her hand hovered over the neck of the garbage bag and she carefully closed her fingers around it.

"Whatever you prefer. Excuse me, I'm just letting myself in."

Granny Ng grabbed the garbage bag, hurried back down the hall into the office, opened the closet door, crouched on the floor behind the plastic boxes, and slid the door shut, breathing in the sharp, acrid smell of mothballs in the dark.

With her cheek against the closet wall, Granny Ng heard the slam of the front door and the young man's wavering voice.

"Sounds good. Great, great. Yes, I'll call you on Wednesday. Me too, very glad."

In the quiet that followed, she imagined the young man stopping on the doormat to slip off his tight office shoes and put them away. She couldn't remember if there was a shoe rack, or if she'd seen pairs of shoes lined up on the floor just inside the door. She thought of her son's cotton-socked toes wedged between the forks of his plastic slippers; a grown man of almost forty, and still his feet looked so childish.

She heard the microwave door open and shut, then a series of beeping sounds. *He's heating up some takeout*, she thought. *He probably eats takeout every night. No wonder the kitchen looks so undisturbed.* The radio came on, a show where people talked about jazz musicians. Then she heard slow, heavy footsteps coming down the corridor towards her. She startled at the sound of a door opening, then realized it was the bathroom door across the hall. A blast of water, quickly muted. More footsteps down the hall—*his steps are very heavy...perhaps he's flat-footed?*—then drawers sliding open and banging lightly against the coasters. The young man was humming something without an obvious melody. His voice was pleasantly soft and light. A high-pitched beep from the microwave echoed down the hall. A blast of water, then muted sounds. The young man had stepped into the steam of the bathroom, ignoring the food that was waiting for him.

Several hours passed before Granny Ng finally heard the door shut on the main bedroom. During those hours, she had listened to the young man's movements over the course of the evening. He'd spent about twenty minutes munching on his dinner in front of his computer before going into the living room and watching a movie. Then he'd returned to the office and started blowing into a musical instrument; it sounded like a small elephant braying. Whatever it was, she thought it must have water in it, the way it wheezed and whistled.

In the closet, she'd found a stack of towels on the shelves and spread several of these on the floor behind the plastic storage boxes. Using the garbage bag she'd filled with supplies as a pillow, she lay down for a few hours. After the first hour or so she became quite stiff and cold from the floor, but apart from that it hadn't been so bad. Finally, upon hearing the bedroom door close, Granny Ng decided it was safe to come out. She stepped out of the closet and stretched her arms and legs.

She decided she would tidy up and sneak out of there while the young man slept. She peered out of the window and saw that the highway was slick with wet. Thinking of her flimsy tent, she hoped it had been a light, brief rain. She had to strain through the dark outside the window to make out her spot in the bushes.

Then it started to pour. Granny Ng sighed. There was nothing for it. She climbed back into the closet, despairing over the state her tent would be in by the morning.

That night, Granny Ng dreamed of her son. Perhaps it was the smell of the mothballs, so pungently antiseptic and reminiscent of the wardrobe in the apartment they'd shared. In what seemed less of a dream than a memory, he appeared to her as a child. She had just picked him up from his first day at school. While children ran past him into their mothers' embraces, he stood hopelessly at the gate, his pale little legs knocking against each other uncertainly.

"I'm taking you for an ice cream for being such a brave boy," she said. His hand was so small and soft in hers, it seemed as though if she squeezed any harder she would crush it like a marshmallow. His fragility, which made her anxious, often brought her to the brink of tears. It took all the restraint she could manage to refrain from coddling him.

In the café, she waited a few minutes for him to enjoy his lemon ice cream before asking, "So, was your first day really as bad as you thought it would be?"

Hesitation flickered across his face; he continued working on his ice cream with greater resolve.

"Is your teacher strict? Or kind?" Her own ice cream was melting in its bowl. "What about your classmates? Did you end up in the same class as your friend Ah Bo?" She regretted how her questions were spoiling his enjoyment of his treat, but she couldn't help probing, urged by the belief that it was better for him to share these things with her.

He scraped the last of the ice cream onto his spoon, gazing at it mournfully as if bidding farewell to a dear friend. Then he turned to her with an anguished look and said, "Why must I go to school?"

She was not prepared for this question. "Why, because... because it's the law." She wished she had come up with a more persuasive answer, but it was the first thing that had come to mind. "Ah, and also of course because you must learn things, and become a smart boy and grow up to be a useful young man. Do you want all the other boys to be better than you?"

She smiled hopefully at her son, appealing to his understanding, and also perhaps his pride, but he was staring at his empty bowl and dragging his spoon back and forth across it. He started tapping it against the bottom of the bowl like a spade hitting a treasure chest in the ground. The sound became loud enough that the other customers in the café started looking over at them.

"Son," she pleaded softly.

Her son continued hitting the spoon against the bowl. Tears welled up in his eyes, and his cheeks were flushed with fearful determination. How had she produced such a sensitive, sullen child, she wondered. As a baby he had seemed so cheerful and full of good nature. She left some money on the table and surprised her son by roughly scooping him up by the armpits and carrying him out of the café, beyond the discreet stares of the other customers, only to have to return moments later to hand over the ice cream spoon to the waitress.

The next morning, Granny Ng waited for the slam of the front door, then hurried out of the closet across the hall, sat on the toilet, and gave a long sigh of relief as she felt the burden she'd been carrying all night leave her body. She stretched her limbs, stiff and aching from sleeping on the cold floor. Then she climbed through the laundry room window with her garbage bag of supplies and crossed the highway towards the bushes. The air was fresh and cool after the night's rain, and the tarmac gleamed in the faint sunshine.

The bushes had been ripped open, the contents of her nest strewn across the ground. The tent covering hung limp from a broken branch; the sleeping bag, bloated with damp like a giant slug, lay underneath it. Granny Ng let herself cry, quietly and briefly. Then she noticed that just a few objects lay on the ground—her clothes, the chopsticks, the tin bowl, and the soaked roll of toilet paper. Her initial distress was replaced by a sense of consolation as she realized it had not been a pointless vandalism; whoever had come to ransack the nest in the night had found things they'd needed. *No one can accuse me of taking up space now,* she thought, gathering up the discarded items. *Not even the bushes or the worms in the ground.* The feeling didn't last long, though; she knew she was fooling herself. The fact remained that her feet were still on this patch of grass; she had not managed to disappear.

Looking over at the young man's house, she made a decision. She crossed back over the highway, unlatched the garden gate, pushed her garbage bag of supplies through the back window, and climbed in after it. After throwing her rain-soaked clothes, sleeping bag, ground mat, and tent cover into the washing machine, she went across the hall into the office and opened the closet doors. The space looked smaller than it had earlier that morning, or the objects in it larger: big plastic storage boxes were stacked three by three in the front, and a row of jackets, trousers, and coats in dry cleaning bags hung above them. All the clothes were wrapped in plastic or folded away in airtight boxes—she guessed that the young man was the kind of person who bought impulsively and accumulated too many of these sweatshirts with logos on the breast or suits that were too mature for him. He probably bought these things out of boredom, or because a co-worker or a girlfriend had encouraged him to.

At the back of the closet, behind the boxes and under the hanging clothes, she contemplated the space where she had slept the night before: roughly two feet wide and five feet long, about three and a half feet between the clothes and the floor. The young man had so much space he didn't have enough to fill it.

Granny Ng couldn't help shaking her head at how much he probably took for granted. She had been raised with the belief that wastefulness was a dire offense; if you had space, you found useful things to occupy it. Her son and daughter-in-law, despite their flaws, knew the value of this—perhaps too well. They had, after all, decided that their space was of more use to them than she was. Granny Ng grimaced at this brief moment of self-pity and turned her attention to her next course of action.

She would make use of that small rectangle of space at the back of the closet, at least until the weather got warm and dry. Then perhaps she would try her luck in another tent village. The idea of moving again immediately nauseated her.

No need to think about it now, she told herself. *Just rest up here for a while and you'll feel more prepared to go out there again.* Pushing the hanging clothes to one side, she looked upon her new home with hopeful imagination. Once her ground mat and sleeping bag had dried, she would lay them down there in the corner with extra towels for bedding, making quite a cozy and comfortable space for herself. It would be like a smaller version of her first tent, but with more insulation than any tent dweller could wish for. Her bag of clothes would sit at her feet, or she could use it as a pillow. Her flashlight had been taken, but what was this? A light cord hung from the ceiling on the left side of the closet. She pulled on it with a click, and the space was filled with a watery yellow glow. As long as the young man was not in the room, she could use this, but otherwise a flashlight would be much better. She would get a toilet roll from the bathroom and lay it next to her head in case she needed to blow her nose in the night. She could deposit her used bits of toilet paper into a plastic bag looped around the handle of one of the boxes. Yes, it would all come together nicely.

To pass the time as she waited for the washing cycle to finish, Granny Ng surveyed the office. She noticed that the computer keyboard had oily keys and guessed that the young man spent a lot of time there. A printer sat next to the computer, paper jutting out of its tray as if sticking its tongue out at her. A black, rectangular case leaned against the corner of the room. She opened it and saw a slim black instrument that had been dismantled and stored in several parts. *So it's a clarinet*, she thought, *not a small elephant, haha.*

She sat in the big, puffy office chair on wheels and scooted around the room for a bit until she started feeling dizzy and had to lie down on the white futon sofa. *Another waste*, she thought. *How well I could use that sofa!* She wondered about the picture of Mount Fuji on the wall—was it somewhere the young man had been to? She didn't recall seeing any photos of him in cold weather clothes. Perhaps it was somewhere he wanted to visit one day, or perhaps he just thought it was pretty. She felt she could understand, as she used to cover her bedroom door with scenic pictures torn from out-of-date calendars: glassy lakes mirroring lush forests, clusters of banyan trees silhouetted by a crimson dusk, cherry blossoms against a blue sky.

As she surveyed the rest of the house, she tried to imagine how a man of so few years could be successful enough to maintain as large and comfortable a home as this. Perhaps he was one of those people who had a gift for computers or business, something like that, or maybe he'd inherited some money.

Upon further investigation, she soon saw through the minimal, ordered appearance of the house. The blinds were full of dust. The metallic sheen of the kitchen cupboards opened to shelves haphazardly stacked with packets of food, crockery, and water bottles. She disapproved of the young man's choice of laundry detergent—too expensive, no brightening agent—and was dismayed to find there was no fabric softener on the shelves. She got on her hands and knees and straightened the thick tatami rug that ran askew along the length of the corridor. In the young man's bedroom, his dresser drawers contained a jumble of socks, underpants, and vests. His wardrobe was no better—clothes squashed together, ties tangled up—and a quick glance under his bed was enough to tell her it was a site of neglect. She was sure she could straighten the place out in a day or two, but knew she couldn't do so without drawing attention to her efforts. So that day she contented herself with taking a damp cloth to the blinds and throwing out some moldy food from the refrigerator. Over the next few days, then weeks, she learned to take a deep breath before opening a drawer or a door and facing the disorder within. Each time she would move just a few things here, a few things there.

JANUARY

Dear Son,

How have you been? I hope you and Daughter-in-law are both in good health. I am sorry if you've been worried about my well-being. I have found a nice place out of town, and I think I will stay here a while. My accommodations are clean and warm, and there is a washer-dryer that makes things very convenient. It is nice here.

The kitchen is well-equipped, although it was terribly disorganized when I first arrived. Pots were with plates, cups and bowls were with packets of food. It really was chaos. I straighten things out a bit here and there because it's the least I can do for my host. He is a young man in his thirties. He has a full-time job, and is often tired when he gets home in the evening. A woman comes on Mondays and Thursdays to clean and run errands, but frankly, she is useless. She gets paid for three hours each time, but she spends only one hour working and the rest of the time she spends on the phone or watching TV. It isn't an exaggeration to say that I do three times as much cleaning as she does. But as I have said, it is the least I can do for my host.

Do you want to hear something funny? The other day

I heard the so-called cleaner talking on the phone. She is convinced that the young man has found himself a girlfriend, and that girlfriend has taken it upon herself to tidy up the place! Meanwhile, the young man noticed how much more organized things had become lately, and he gave the cleaner a small raise and thanked her for all her hard work. What a shock this must have been for her! You can imagine how popular this imaginary girlfriend is with her.

Although I make light of it, I really would like to see him with a nice young woman. Lately there has been someone he talks to a lot on the phone, but she doesn't seem right for him. He always sounds as if he's apologizing or trying to calm her down. She came here one evening after they'd been out for dinner. I could hear her voice all the way from the living room. She was complaining about a waitress she thought had been rude to her at the restaurant. "For such a high-class place they hire really low-class staff," were her words. I thought she must be very beautiful for him to put up with such an ugly temperament. I was right. A week or so later he put a framed picture of her in the office, next to his computer. She looked like a movie star, long hair, very pretty.

When the lazy cleaner isn't around and the young man is at work or out on the weekends with his young woman, I have the whole place to myself. This is my favorite time. I usually try to find something to keep myself busy. Today I took down the curtains and washed and ironed them. Yesterday I collected the young man's socks and darned the ones that looked like they were starting to get holes in them. I don't mind it at all.

I relax by practicing Tai Chi in the garden. It's also been nice to catch up on some TV shows. Remember I used to follow that soap opera set in a countryside clinic? I stopped watching it for a few months and now everything's different—new actors are playing old characters, people are married or divorced or dead. I can barely keep up; everything's changed so quickly. Fortunately, real life moves a little more slowly.

I wish you could see what a nice place this is.

Please take care of yourself,
Your mother

FEBRUARY

Granny Ng could not understand why the grass in the garden seemed not to have grown during the time she'd been there. She pressed her palms lightly against the blades; they felt real enough. The sparseness of the garden made it seem like something no one wanted to care for or devote any time or thought to, and this made her feel sad for it. She started imagining a row of orchids here, a fishpond there, sometimes drawing variations of these ideas on sheets of printer paper. It was a strangely liberating feeling; she hadn't drawn for years and was amazed to find that her hands were still somewhat faithful to her imagination, and that she was still capable of rendering the images in her mind. Sometimes, when she tired of drawing gardens, she drew animals. Later on she attempted reproductions of famous paintings, but found that her memory often failed her in the details. She taped all of these drawings, finished or not, to the side and back walls of the closet, where they hung over her sleeping head like dreams in waiting.

Dear Son,

The weather is turning cooler. How have you been? The more I think about it the more I find similarities between you and this young man. You are both tidy but not very clean. You both dislike bananas and enjoy music. He plays the clarinet. He plays it once in the morning after his shower and once in the evening before bed. He never plays an entire tune. He usually plays scales, or practices the same part of a song over and over again, maybe fifteen or twenty times. It gives me a bit of a headache to tell you the truth. You are more gifted musically. You played the flute very well. It's a shame you gave it up after high school.

But there are also differences. You are up and out of the apartment in less than forty-five minutes. He takes an hour and a half. At 6:30 am the radio comes on in his bedroom and in the kitchen, a jazz station that plays very energetic music. He always walks to the bathroom singing or humming whatever song is playing that morning. If he's in a good mood, he'll sing loudly in the shower. That cheers me up. When I use the bathroom after him, it smells of cucumber and mint and is full of condensation. I have to turn on the extractor fan, open the window, and hang up the bath mat to dry.

Straight after his shower, he goes into the office and plays the clarinet for about ten or fifteen minutes. I can hardly bear it, not so much because of the noise but because I think he's going to catch a cold. Of course it's not my place to tell him what to do, but I don't understand why he can't wait till he's put some clothes on. Maybe once he's dressed for work, he's no longer in the mood to play.

Like you, he enjoys his coffee. The kitchen always smells of it after he leaves. He has a cup in the kitchen while he watches the breakfast news on TV, then he pours the rest into a flask, which he takes to work. As he gathers up his things, he starts on an apple, and I can hear him crunching all the way from the end of the hall. I think a young man should have more than coffee and an apple in the mornings, but who knows—maybe he has a big, hearty lunch at work.

I hope you and Daughter-in-law are well. Remember not to work too hard, and be sure to eat lots of warming food as the weather gets cooler—lots of ginger and garlic. Make some soup. Please give Maru my love.

Take care of yourself,
Your mother

Granny Ng noticed that the young man often brought home takeout dinners or ate instant ramen in the evening. That morning apple seemed to be the only healthy thing he ate. She wanted to cook for him, to encourage him to eat more, but the only feasible way of doing this was by using the cleaner as a cover. Every Monday and Thursday at eleven o'clock the cleaner would let herself in. Thursdays there would be a white envelope of cash with *Mrs. Lee* written on the front stuck to the door of the fridge. By two o'clock the cleaner would leave and the envelope would be gone from the fridge door, an instructive note in its place: "Mr. Mok, Please remember to leave money for milk, eggs, and rice" or "Mr. Mok, Usual detergent out of stock, different brand costs extra 15 HKD. Please add amount to envelope."

After practicing the cleaner's handwriting, Granny Ng left a note on the fridge door: "Mr. Mok, Curried vegetables and rice in fridge. Cover dish with glass lid. Microwave three minutes." The next morning, Granny Ng was pleased to find a dirty plate in the dishwasher and no leftovers in the trash. After the second dish—"Fried snapper with scrambled egg and tomato. Splash a little water on egg and tomato. Microwave 1 minute"—she was surprised to find a Post-it note on the fridge door:

Dear Mrs. Lee, I enjoyed the food.
Thank you, you are too kind.

Granny Ng felt a flush of happiness, then panic. She tore the note from the fridge door, crumpled it up and threw it in the trash. Then, fearing he might find it in there and take offense, she fished it out, smoothed it open, and stuck it on the back wall of her closet next to her drawings. The young man made a habit of leaving a thank you Post-it on the fridge each time a dish had been left for him, even when Granny Ng knew he hadn't enjoyed it so much (the next morning she might find half of it in the trash, along with an empty ramen noodle packet). Granny Ng dutifully collected these thank you notes and found a place for each one on the closet wall among her drawings, where they gradually spread like vine leaves. Occasionally one would peel off in the night, and she'd wake to find it resting on her forehead or cheek.

MARCH

Dear Son,

How have you been? I'm glad that everything has worked out for both of us. Things are going well here, and with the extra room you now have, you and Daughter-in-law can start thinking about having a baby. It's a shame your father isn't here to see you move into this phase of life.

Granny Ng put down the pen. She struggled to conjure up her late husband's face, absentmindedly stroking the thin silver band on her finger. It had lost its shine over the years and was now a foggy grey, bearing a closer resemblance to tin than silver. She had never thought of selling it, not even at her most desperate; it had just never occurred to her, just as it wouldn't have occurred to her to cut off her finger or ear and imagine it would be of any value to anybody else.

She couldn't see her husband's face, but she could feel the flat, smooth plane of the back of his head against her palm. She had held it every day towards the end, helping him keep his head up as she spooned warm broth into his mouth. As a child he had been affectionately nicknamed "Flatheaded Boy" by everyone in the village. She had never given much thought to this feature of his, and was surprised to think of it now. Over the years, her memories of him had appeared in increasingly broad strokes: his narrow, thoughtful face; his stubbornness; his pale, weakening body that smelled of old bread; her quiet despair at being left alone just a year after her son was born. She stroked the creases of her palm, and for a moment wondered if she had remembered correctly—if her memory of the flat back of her husband's head had not in fact been that of her infant son's.

* * *

Granny Ng heard the young man pacing about the room. She curled up tighter. She was waiting for him to curse or slam a door or break a glass. Although she knew it wasn't like him to lose his temper, she waited for the sound of something nevertheless. But all she heard was the clink and groan of the ironing board being folded up, the static hiss of a machine coming to life. Click. Click.

Another evening alone at his computer. The quiet was occasionally interrupted by a voice or an advertising jingle—an announcement that he'd won a million dollars or an invitation to join a fun party by dialing this number. Then sound effects—a rippling of cards, plastic chips clinking against each other, the dealer's catchphrase, "The house always wins—but maybe not tonight!"

Granny Ng recognized the game. Her son used to play online poker until his wife found out and forced him to transfer all of his money to their joint account. The sound effects continued for some time, and from the increasingly frequent exclamations from the dealer—"You're really cleaning up!" and "You've got the moves!"—Granny Ng surmised that he was on a winning streak. She felt happy for him: at least he had some consolation for the disappointments of the evening. Earlier, he had taken out a new shirt and ironed his pants, even opening a new tube of gel in an attempt to mold his hair. A few days before, Granny Ng had heard him on the phone with the young woman, agreeing that he needed to give his hair "some personality." Still, it appeared as if the young woman had decided she didn't want to spend the evening with him for some reason. Granny Ng had listened as he tried to sound understanding, saying that no, he hadn't gone through a lot of trouble. She'd listened as he called to cancel the restaurant, as he washed the gel out of his hair in the bathroom sink, as he shoved the plate of food she'd made for him into the microwave. But now he was winning money online, and amidst the clamor of sound effects, she could hear him say, "Yes! Yes!"

She was happy for him, but her happiness would have been greater were she not in such desperate need of the toilet. Her bladder, she felt, was the only thing about her age that betrayed her in this situation, the only inconvenience. In an effort to reduce the frequency of her urination, she had taken to drinking only two glasses of water a day. It seemed to have some effect during the daytime—she only needed to use the toilet twice—but after 7 pm, when the young man returned and she had to stow herself away in the closet, the urge to urinate would visit her two to three times during the night. She'd made this discovery the hard way; on one of her first nights there, she had brought an empty half-liter water bottle and a funnel with her into the closet. This served its purpose until she woke in the middle of night with both a bladder and a bottle that needed to be emptied. She'd had to open the closet door, tiptoe to the window, and trickle the contents of the bottle onto the lawn before she could use it again. After that, she always brought a second half-liter bottle into the closet with her. In the mornings, after the young man had left for work, Granny Ng would go to the bathroom and disinfect the bottles and the funnel, filling them with diluted detergent and setting them under the taps in the bathtub for thirty minutes before rinsing them out.

Granny Ng clutched the empty bottle in the dark, hoping she could wait it out. Usually when the young man was at his computer in the evenings, she would time her toilet breaks with his; so far this solution had worked without complications. But this evening, the young man was not doing his part.

The telephone started ringing from down the hall. The young man continued playing his game. Granny Ng silently pleaded with him, *Please go to the phone, it might be that young woman! Maybe she's come to her senses and wants to tell you she's sorry! Please answer the phone, if only to give her a piece of your mind!*

The dealer congratulated him again—"Expertly played!" A few more telephone rings, then silence. Granny Ng sank into despair, and her sympathetic feelings for the young man turned into sharp annoyance. Then she heard his chair roll across the floor and his footsteps leaving the room. Granny Ng seized the moment and quickly unscrewed the bottle cap.

Granny Ng had been holding on for so long that when the time came to urinate, she missed the top of the funnel at first and got the floor of the closet instead. She reproached herself as she mopped up the wet patch with a towel from the shelf. *How many times have you done this now!* Footsteps again; the chair squeaked under the young man's weight. For the next few minutes Granny Ng heard little except the hum of the computer, the swish of cars passing on the freeway, and some occasional clicks. *He's probably had enough of the poker,* she thought. She was glad he'd quit while he was ahead. Maybe he was reading the news now. She leaned her head against the wall and closed her eyes. She thought about the scrapbook she used to keep for saving her favorite news articles. These were often unusual or uplifting stories, such as the Japanese family vacationing in Kyoto who lost their beloved dog in an amusement park, returned heartbroken to Osaka, and a week later were amazed to find the dog sitting on their doorstep, having miraculously found its way home. In another article, a sixty-three year old British man who'd been blind his entire life claimed to have regained his sight after traveling to Italy and catching his first whiff of pizza.

Granny Ng had kept a special section in her scrapbook devoted to tales of reunited families. Her favorite stories concerned twins who'd been separated at a young age and then reunited under fantastically coincidental circumstances after twenty, thirty, forty years. She thought of the woman from Tokyo who was honeymooning in Niagara Falls with her husband. Lunching at their hotel restaurant overlooking the falls, the woman spilled wine on her blouse and went up to their room to change. Her husband stayed at their table to finish his glass of wine, and, after a few minutes, decided to visit the seafood buffet. Seeing his wife examine the oyster-shaped ice sculpture, he snuck up behind her, grabbed her waist, and planted a kiss on her neck. He was alarmed by her screams, and couldn't understand why she was shouting at him in English. He was even more alarmed by the angry-looking blonde man approaching them. His confusion deepened when another woman who looked just like his wife joined in, demanding to know what was going on.

From this confusing encounter, the truth emerged: the two women were twin sisters who'd been separated at birth after their parents' divorce. One had been raised by their mother in Tokyo, the other by their father in Boston. The sisters were both architects, enjoyed ice-skating, and had married their co-workers (also both architects). And both of them had chosen to honeymoon in Niagara Falls. After the accidental reunion, the sisters called each other every day and visited each other twice a year. Their mother had died years before, but their father was still alive. When he met his long-lost daughter, it was the first time in his life that he'd wept in front of another person.

Another memorable story concerned a young married couple who were featured on a medical TV show in Germany. They wanted to get pregnant, so they took a screening test to rule out the possibility of genetic defects in their future child. This couple believed that they were made for each other. They had met at the same company (both were engineers), had the same taste in food and music, and even had the same allergies. The screening test revealed why they were such a perfect match; over a quarter of their genes were the same. They eventually discovered that both of their mothers had lived in the same neighborhood and had received sperm from the same donor to conceive a child. At the time, the procedure was very new and there were very few sperm donors available, so sperm banks gave out the same donors in the same area. Confronted with the knowledge that they were half-siblings, and facing enormous societal pressure, the couple split up. However, six months later, rumors surfaced of the couple reuniting and running away to England.

The article had ended there, but Granny Ng longed to know more. She wanted to know what had become of them, if they had succeeded in eluding their interfering families and friends. Perhaps they'd assumed new identities? Would this mean they wouldn't be able to get the same kind of work? Or maybe they had a sympathetic boss who helped connect them with another engineering firm in England. And what about children? Despite her concerns, Granny Ng liked to imagine that the couple was living quietly and happily in their newfound anonymity. She wished she hadn't listened to Kitty, who had made her leave the scrapbook behind when she was helping her pack for the tent village. "Don't worry, Granny. You can collect more stories," she'd told her.

Granny Ng didn't know how long she'd been asleep. She came around to the faint smell of urine and the sound of a woman gasping thirstily for air. A man's grunts and moans joined the woman's gasps, which got faster and throatier. A prickly warmth spread across Granny Ng's cheeks and she covered her ears, then stuck her fingers in them, after which she could only hear the thumping of her pulse. After a few minutes of this, she took her fingers out of her ears. The sounds had completely ceased. She wondered if the young man had left the room. Then it came—his quiet, crushing moan like a wounded animal in its death throes.

The next morning, Granny Ng found that she'd woken up half an hour earlier than usual and that the closet reeked of urine. She stuffed some tissue paper into her nostrils and crossed her arms tightly as she waited for the young man to get up and out of the house. As she listened to the noises that had become so familiar by now—the jazz station on the radio, his singing, the blast of the shower, the clarinet squeakily climbing scales—each one felt like a minor affront, painfully drawing out the moments she had to spend next to the urine-caked towel.

At the slam of the front door, Granny Ng got up and filled a bucket with warm soapy water, moved the plastic storage boxes and her sleeping bag out of the way, and started scrubbing the closet floor, becoming increasingly agitated with the effort. In just a few minutes she had grown uncomfortably hot, and her back and elbows were aching.

For the rest of the day, she tried to go about her normal routine, washing the dishes or wiping down a cabinet, but she found herself suddenly filled with the dreadful sense that these experiences did not wholly belong to her. These dishes were not hers, nor was the cabinet, nor the cloth in her hand. No one even knew she was doing any of this.

"All this effort," she muttered, "and for what?" It took a great force of will to finish each chore, and finally she gave up. The tasks she had once been eager to do now felt like a punishment, a sentence.

The lazy cleaner was coming today. When Granny Ng took her place inside the closet just before eleven o'clock, she was surprised by the sudden violence of her feelings toward Mrs. Lee.

"I do your work, and then I hide myself in here while you laze about. What use on this earth do you have?!"

Half an hour after the arrival of Mrs. Lee, during which Granny Ng imagined the woman halfheartedly dragging a cloth across the kitchen counters and stealing snacks from the fridge, the phone rang. Granny Ng heard her speak quite animatedly for about five minutes to the person at the other end, then her loud, grating laugh and the sound of the front door slamming. After waiting a while, Granny Ng came out of her hiding place and looked around. The cleaner had left a note on the fridge door for the young man: "Mr. Mok, My apologies. Must leave a few minutes early today. Son called home sick from school. Usual chores taken care of. Thank you."

It was unnecessary for her to leave the note—the young man would have no idea when she'd actually come and gone—but she liked to do things like this to appear more honest than she actually was. That was one of the many small, subtle deceits that seemed to be second nature to the woman. From the beginning, this had struck Granny Ng as arrogant and disrespectful, and she had made a point of disposing of such notes whenever the cleaner felt compelled to leave one. This time, though, she left Mrs. Lee's note on the fridge door and had a cup of tea on the sofa. *Let him be deceived*, she thought. *I can't always be looking out for him.*

She picked up the remote control and turned on the television. Immediately the faces and voices made her feel a little better. During the course of the day, she watched a cooking program, a talk show, a travel show, a wildlife documentary, and a drama set in a police academy. She only got up from the sofa to use the toilet and get an apple from the kitchen. By the time she realized she'd forgotten to make any food for herself, it was too late; the young man was due to return at any minute. Granny Ng went to sleep hungry, annoyed at how she'd let time slip away from her and feeling nauseous from all the TV she'd watched that day.

APRIL

It was not enough to live among the objects and habits of another person; she needed to sit down with someone over a cup of hot tea and bean cake. She tried to distract herself by reinvesting her attention towards fixing things around the house: darning the young man's socks, washing the blinds, the windows, leaving him dinner twice a week. But still she missed the company of friends.

She pulled a few maps down from the bookshelf and began looking for the location of her first tent village, where Kitty and Uncle Chow had taken her in. At the time she still hadn't fully warmed to the experience of communal living, everyone in such close quarters and knowing each other's business. But now she looked back on that time with a regretful appreciation and longing.

It took her some time to work out a route from the young man's house to the tent village, and she was a little disheartened to find that it was farther than she'd imagined. It would take almost an hour and a half and require three route changes to get there by bus. She was determined, however, to make the journey.

She decided she would go the next day. She had enough money for the bus fare; she had not yet spent any of what she'd made from begging and collecting recyclables while living at the last tent village. The problem was figuring out what to bring. She couldn't drop by both unannounced and empty-handed. In the end, she managed to cobble together a satisfactory gift bag and went to sleep that night more contented than she'd felt in a long time.

Kitty and Uncle Chow were surprised and happy to see her, but unable to completely hide their concern.

"Is everything okay, Granny?" they asked. "Did you get evicted again?"

"No, no. I'm fine," said Granny Ng. "I just wanted to pay you a visit. I'm sorry I didn't give you any notice."

"Are you sure you're okay? Do you have somewhere to stay?" asked Kitty.

"Yes, yes, a very good place," said Granny Ng. "If you don't believe me, look."

She opened up the plastic garbage bag full of gifts and laid out the contents on the ground: a barely used towel, two bars of soap, four tins of pork cubes, four packets of instant ramen, a packet of AA batteries, three airline cosmetics bags with face cloths, razors, toothbrushes, and cotton buds, and half a bottle of laundry detergent.

"That's all for you," said Granny Ng. "If I had nowhere to stay, I'd be standing here with a bag full of my own things, wouldn't I?"

"Well, I feel reassured," said Uncle Chow.

"Thank you for these things, Granny. You really shouldn't have," said Kitty. Granny Ng noticed that Kitty didn't seem that pleased, and she tried not to be upset by her friend's lack of enthusiasm. She sensed there must be something else going on.

Granny Ng's first impression upon arriving in the tent village was that not much had changed. She'd found Uncle Chow cooking soup on the stove and Kitty in a bright blue tracksuit at her tent a few spots over, cutting someone's hair and chatting animatedly. The only noticeable difference was that there seemed to be slightly fewer tents.

Uncle Chow handed her a bowl of soup. "Careful, it's hot."

"Beef?" asked Granny Ng.

"Vegetable," said Uncle Chow. "I'm trying to lose weight." He winked and patted his stomach. It was then that Granny Ng noticed: his cheeks had a hollowness that she hadn't seen before, and the silver specks in his beard seemed to have dulled.

"Times are getting tougher," sighed Kitty. "The butcher used to give us his off-cuts for cheap, and the grocer would give us a good deal on rice and tinned food. We used to have friends around here. But last month, city officials did another sweep of the area. They not only evicted thirteen residents, they also went to the local businesses that were helping us and threatened them with fines."

Uncle Chow shot a scowl at Kitty for revealing so much of their situation. He cleared his throat and smiled at Granny Ng.

"And you, Granny?" he asked. "You seem to be in very good health."

"How are things at the other tent village?" asked Kitty.

Granny Ng shook her head. "I was evicted from there not long after I arrived."

"Oh dear!" said Kitty.

"I went to another village. But I had to leave there, too, after a while. And then another village. I suppose I didn't have much luck in those places."

"But you seem fine now," said Uncle Chow. "Did you go back to your son's? Is this where you got all these things?"

Granny Ng looked at Uncle Chow's thinned face and at Kitty, still so well-meaning and eager to help. They didn't really know each other that well, and actually had little in common. However, they were the first people in years that she'd considered her friends, and she wanted to be honest with them. She wondered how she could explain her situation. On the one hand, it would be a relief to share her secret, and perhaps they would be pleased for her. On the other hand, she might be burdening them with this information. Kitty in particular would doubtless overlook the benefits of her situation, focusing instead on the risks and trying to persuade her to leave the young man's home before she got into trouble.

"Yes," said Granny Ng. "I'm living at my son's again. Don't worry, he knows that I took all these things, and he's very glad to help. Things are much better between us now."

After that, Granny Ng made sure to visit Kitty and Uncle Chow every few weeks. Each time she would bring something for them, usually tins of food or fruit. But she knew the really useful items—firewood, gasoline—were too much for her to carry by herself. Eventually she started looking around the house for money that the young man had absentmindedly left around.

On the kitchen counter was a large glass jar full of coins where he would throw his loose change, pulling it from his trouser and jacket pockets on his way in from work. It was a little over half full, and every week Granny Ng would notice a small dip where the cleaner had scooped out a few coins. Not enough to attract the young man's notice, but enough, Granny Ng supposed, to make it worth her while. Granny Ng thought that she could probably get away with taking a few coins as well. She felt guilty about this, and a little ashamed. But she told herself it was for a good cause, and that failing to share her good fortune with her less fortunate friends would be an even greater crime.

After three weeks, she had collected a little over 200 HKD. She took this money to Kitty and Uncle Chow, who refused to accept it, claiming they were already uncomfortable enough accepting her gifts. Although disappointed, Granny Ng felt it was important to relieve this awkwardness and did not insist. Instead, she began taking small electrical items from the house—a flashlight, a calculator, a hand-held fan—and dropping them on the ground, shaking them, or throwing water on them. Then she would take them to Uncle Chow to repair. Uncle Chow reluctantly accepted these jobs, but only after Granny Ng told him that if he didn't, her son and daughter-in-law would find out about her clumsiness and get angry with her. He also insisted that she take a flask of soup back with her after each visit. She began adding the soup to the meals she left in the fridge for the young man, whose thank you notes the following day became increasingly appreciative.

But as dedicated as Granny Ng was to helping her friends, she knew the visits were as much for her as for them. She looked forward to seeing them every few weeks, bringing food or supplies or more damaged electrical items. While Uncle Chow worked on a newly battered radio or electric kettle, Granny Ng would make soup in the communal kitchen, or drink tea and chat with Kitty while she cooked lunch or cut a neighbor's hair. In the summer, she helped sew a new lining for Kitty's tent and had Kitty cut her hair cut into a neat bob that let her feel a pleasant coolness on the back of her neck.

OCTOBER

In the second week of October, the local homeless coalition held a community fair in the park. There were over twenty different stalls offering free hair cuts, vaccines, basic medical check ups and eye tests that the villagers could visit. Although Granny Ng could no longer claim to be a tent villager, she managed with Kitty's help to get a free pair of reading glasses and a medical check up. (Aside from slightly low blood pressure, the doctor gave her a clean bill of health.) Uncle Chow had to be persuaded by Kitty to get a check up, and was told he had high cholesterol and blood pressure. "I don't see the use of being told these things if you can't do anything about them," he grumbled.

Kitty persuaded Granny Ng to stay for the barbecue party. Granny Ng acquiesced, but urged Kitty to go and chat with her neighbors; she wasn't feeling particularly sociable, and was happy to sit and listen to the music playing from the stereo. She settled herself on a plastic stool and nibbled slowly on a single chicken kebab, balancing a paper bowl of soup on her lap. She had felt fine about getting free tests and a pair of glasses from the fair, but now she suddenly felt like an interloper taking from the needy. It was best, she thought, to stay on the sidelines and not draw attention to herself.

Her plan was not successful. Tent village residents and coalition volunteers kept coming up to her and asking if they could get her anything, why was she eating so little, did she need a blanket? Finally, the only way to reassure them and deflect their attention was to accept their food-laden plates and pretend she was chewing whenever they checked up on her.

Brother Shek, the construction worker, greeted Granny Ng and took a seat next to her. He was carrying a short-necked lute. "Nice to see you again, Granny. Maybe I've had one too many beers, but I'm in such a good mood that I have to inflict my playing on our friends. You don't mind, do you?"

Granny Ng shook her head, surprising herself with a giggle that was almost girlish. Brother Shek stood up and announced, "I hope no one objects to my amateurish playing," to which villagers responded with enthusiastic cheers. Brother Shek started playing and leading the others in renditions of popular folk songs and theme tunes from old television serials. At Brother Shek's invitation, Kitty got up and sang the solo of one of these songs, startling Granny Ng with the melodiousness of her voice. The crowd urged her to sing again and again. She was a confident and theatrical performer, urging the villagers to clap along and pausing to tease several of them with a song's romantic lyrics. Kitty received her standing ovation with the effortless grace of a seasoned performer.

Brother Shek leaned over to Granny Ng and said, "It's a shame she doesn't sing more often. I hear she used to be a regular on the hotel circuit. Now it's all karaoke machines."

"I thought she was a hairdresser," said Granny Ng.

"She *was*," said Brother Shek's wife, who had taken the seat beside Granny Ng unnoticed. She looked a little plumper than before, though it might have been the billowy floral shirt she was wearing.

"She just sang for fun," Brother Shek's wife asserted. "She never made it as a real singer."

When Kitty came back to the group, she was a little breathless and excited, her face flushed with pink. "I hope I didn't make a nuisance of myself out there," she smiled.

"We were saying what a shame it is that you don't sing for us more often," said Brother Shek.

"You have a very smooth voice," added Granny Ng.

"You're so kind," said Kitty. "It's nice to have an appreciative audience."

At the request of her neighbors, Kitty agreed to an encore. She chose a song that Granny Ng recognized as having been popular in the seventies. As Kitty sang, the melodious strains of her voice spun and floated up towards the late afternoon sky like an invocation to an unknown god.

DECEMBER

On the third day of December, Granny Ng was caught and arrested. The young man had installed a surveillance system whose cameras had recorded the movements of a small elderly woman wandering around his house. The police found her in the closet, curled up on her side. She looked up nervously at the police officers, a middle-aged male and a younger female, who stared back in surprise. Finally, the female officer called the young man in from the living room.

"Looks like we've found your burglar, sir."

The female police officer—she introduced herself as Officer Wong—helped Granny Ng up and apologized for having to place cuffs on her, then asked her to sit down on the white futon sofa. The young man stood by the computer table, regarding Granny Ng warily as if she were a wild animal. She avoided the young man's stare, though she would have liked nothing better than to get a proper look at him. As Officer Wong surveyed the inside of the closet, she said to her colleague, "Officer Tang, would you like to begin?"

Officer Tang stood over Granny Ng scratching his balding head and seemingly at a loss for words. Finally, he squatted down in front of her and said, "Granny, are you comfortable?"

Granny Ng nodded. "Quite comfortable, thank you. But these handcuffs…"

"Yes, I'm sorry about that," said Officer Tang. He pulled a slim notebook and pen from his jacket pocket, then tapped the pad a few times before asking, "Do you realize, Granny, that you've broken the law?"

Granny Ng bit her lip. She stared at the edge of a small, half-moon indent in the carpet where one of the computer table legs had shifted.

"This is private property," he continued, "belonging to this gentleman here. If Mr. Mok decides to press charges—"

"Why did you say my name?!" exclaimed the young man at a volume that seemed to surprise even himself.

"I think it's a bit late for that," said Officer Wong, peeling a Post-it note from the closet wall. "I imagine she knows quite a lot about you already."

Officer Tang continued. "If Mr. Mok decides to move forward, you could be charged with counts of housebreaking, trespassing—"

"And theft," added the young man.

"What items have been stolen, Mr. Mok?" asked Officer Wong.

"Well, food, mostly."

"*Mostly?* Anything else? Anything of value?"

The young man hesitated, then shook his head.

"I see." Officer Tang noted this in his book, then stood up and rubbed his knees, which were sore from the squatting. "Granny, my colleague and I here need to fill out a report, and for that we need to ask you some simple questions. It would be much better if you could cooperate with us on this."

Granny Ng nodded.

"Good. Now, can you please tell me your full name?"

"Ng Shui Lin."

"Age?"

"Sixty-three. No, wait—sixty-four."

"How long have you been living here?"

Granny Ng finally stole a glance at the young man, who was staring at the wall over her shoulder with an expression of nervousness and quiet anger.

She answered quietly. "One year."

"What!" The young man was almost shouting, his face reddened. "Why did you do this? Is this your idea of fun? Why aren't you at home with your children and grandchildren? Do they even know where you are?"

The officers asked the young man to calm down and suggested that they continue the investigation at the station.

Granny Ng and the young man were each interviewed for half an hour. The young man told Officer Tang that for the past few months, he'd begun to notice that food was going missing. He also noticed that household supplies like soap and toilet paper were getting used up a lot more quickly than usual. At first he'd thought little of it, putting it down to his own absentmindedness; perhaps Mrs. Lee the cleaner had left him a note about it and he'd forgotten. After all, he would also lose track of other things:

he'd forget where he'd put a flashlight or an extension cable, for example, and then after a few weeks the items would just turn up on their own. But after some time, a vague, nagging doubt began to visit him just before falling asleep at night. The following morning, before leaving for work, he would quickly check around the house for signs of disturbance. He never found any.

Again he tried to put his uneasiness down to paranoia, reasoning that he'd probably been working too hard and spending too much time alone. But once in a while he would check the rooms, the cupboards, the closets. Though he never found anything, that nagging sense of doubt continued to visit him at night. During the weekends, at certain times of the day, he would get the feeling that he was not alone. The surveillance system had been expensive, but it gave him some peace of mind. He said he only wished he'd thought of it sooner.

By the time the officers had finished their interrogation, the young man had learned some more details about the old woman: that she was homeless and had broken into his home the previous winter, set up a sleeping space for herself in the spare closet, and managed to live there undetected for a year. He found this difficult to accept, as he was sure he'd checked that closet, but then admitted that yes, perhaps in his haste he hadn't bothered to push the hanging clothes aside to check behind the plastic storage boxes. He also learned that she'd spent her days cooking, cleaning, doing chores around the house, and getting electrical items repaired for him. His cleaner had not, as he'd believed, had a surge of conscientiousness.

After coming home from the police station, he opened up the closet and, overcoming feelings of queasiness, gathered the old woman's things into a garbage bag. There wasn't much there—a sleeping bag, some clothes, two empty water bottles, a thin stack of letters addressed to her son, and some drawings and Post-it notes lining the walls.

Ken Mok spent the following week in a state of indignation and embarrassment. He wanted to share the burden of his victimization with other people—his father, his co-workers, the woman who no longer wanted to speak to him—but decided against it. His father would see this incident as further proof of his son's stupidity and incompetence. *How can a person not know that a stranger is living in their house? For a year!* His co-workers would no doubt see this as a ripe opportunity for ridicule. The day after the arrest, short articles had appeared in several newspapers, identifying the young man as "A 33-year old I.T. professional. The old woman was identified as Ng Shui Lin, 64 years old. The woman appeared to be of normal mental health. When police asked her why she had lived in secrecy at the man's home for a year, she replied, 'I had nowhere to live.'"

A few days later, a colleague emailed him an article about the incident, which someone else had sent him from a news website. The subject line read, *How Dumb Is This Guy?* Mr. Mok assured himself that this wasn't directed at him personally. It would be impossible for anyone to know the true details of the incident; there must be hundreds of thirty-three-year-old I.T. professionals living in the area. He searched the story online and found that brief articles had appeared in some sixty-seven news outlets, comprised largely of websites from China. To his relief, he found that in all of these, he remained anonymous.

After some time, and he thought, an unusual amount of

persuasion from the police officers handling the case, Mr. Mok decided to drop the charges against the old woman. The officers managed to convince him that she posed no real danger to him, and that they would make sure she was returned to the care of her son and daughter-in-law. Immediately after agreeing to drop the charges, Mr. Mok installed a more advanced security system in his home. Any instance of the alarm going off would send an alert straight to his cell phone, so that even at work he could feel reassured.

Mr. Mok tried to return to his old routines with the same normalcy and thoughtlessness as before, but found that a new, nagging feeling had replaced the old one. This new feeling manifested itself as a dense weight in his lungs, like a cloud of stone, and seemed to appear at odd, inexplicable moments: when he set foot in the house after work; when he stepped out of the steam of the bathroom; when he dropped a cake of ramen noodles into a pan of boiling water. This gradually affected his posture, and he developed a slight stoop.

From time to time, he opened the closet door and peered inside. It still seemed unbelievable to him that a person could have stowed herself away there for all that time. The inhumanity of it both saddened and repulsed him. There was no longer any trace of a stranger having lived there, and this unnerved him more than if he'd found some scrap of evidence—a hair pin, say, or a stray button.

He had trouble sleeping. He would wake in the middle of the night and feverishly check the closet, then the doors and windows, even the cupboards. After a few weeks, the house had fallen into its former state of subtle disarray. His habit of looking for things and expecting to find them in their right places was gradually undermined by his tendency to distractedly throw things in any available cupboard or drawer space. One day, upon arriving home, he noticed a brief moment of disappointment when he saw there was no Post-it note on the fridge, and realized that he'd hoped this act of care and attention had somehow magically transferred to Mrs. Lee.

Eventually Mr. Mok acknowledged how much the old woman had been taking care of things, and how little Mrs. Lee had been doing all these years. He fired her and placed an advert for her replacement in the local classifieds. The next day, he called the newspaper to withdraw the advert, deciding he would rather not have another stranger in his house. The house fell into further disarray. That dense, weighted feeling grew stronger, and the stoop of his back grew a little deeper, so that he had the air of someone perpetually cold.

One Saturday morning, Mr. Mok phoned the police station and asked for the officers in charge of the case. Officer Wong took his call. She could barely conceal her surprise, and was guarded when answering his questions about the old woman. Finally, after several minutes of assuring her of his benign intentions, she told him to come down to the station. There, she and Officer Tang told him that soon after the old woman's arrest, a search had gone out for her next of kin (she had refused to tell them the whereabouts of her son, claiming she had forgotten). It was outside of their normal scope of involvement, but the officers felt badly for the old woman, and had posted an appeal for her relatives to contact the police.

After a week with no reply, during which the old woman had been placed in a shelter, Officer Wong managed to track down the old woman's son and daughter-in-law. They claimed to have been completely ignorant of the situation. When questioned about their lack of action at the time of her disappearance, they said that she'd left a note about visiting a relative. They added that they'd received a letter from her some time later, informing them of her decision to live at a friend's house, and that she was quite happy there.

"The funny thing," said Officer Tang, "is that they looked like such a nice, respectable sort of couple on the surface. He's a teacher, and she works for one of those fashion places—"

"Louis Vuitton," said Officer Wong. "But nothing too exciting; she works in the accounting department."

"They just didn't look like the kind of people who'd let their own mother wander the streets," said Officer Tang.

"If you don't mind me asking," said Officer Wong, "why exactly are you trying to find her?"

"I just want to make sure she's all right," said Mr. Mok, surprised to hear the words come out of his words. "Believe it or not, I feel a little responsible." Before he could help himself, he blurted out, "I was thinking of giving her a job."

The police officers looked dubious.

"As a housekeeper," he continued. "She did a good job of keeping the place in order. I suppose I never fully appreciated it at the time." As soon as he heard himself say it out loud, it really didn't seem like such a bad idea.

The police officers told him the son and daughter-in-law had placed her in a nursing home, which, in the end, meant that she was probably no better off than if they'd never been tracked down. "You know the kinds of things that happen in there," said Officer Wong.

By the time Mr. Mok left the station, the two officers had helped him find the name and number of the nursing home. He called that day, pretending to be the old woman's son. The receptionist sounded surprised to hear from him. He asked if he could visit her that day. The receptionist told him that visiting hours were over, and when he asked if he could come by the next morning, she informed him that the home needed at least twenty-four hours' notice to prepare the residents for visitors.

"What do you mean, *prepare?*" asked Mr. Mok.

The receptionist responded with an edge of impatience to her voice. "Some of our residents have very particular needs. We prefer to avoid making family members distressed, particularly young children. Some of our residents have difficulty controlling their behavior."

"Well, it's just me, and I don't mind," said Mr. Mok.

"It's company policy," snapped the receptionist. Then, in a gentler, rehearsed voice, "Please call at least twenty-four hours in advance to schedule a visit. Thank you."

She hung up before Mr. Mok could reply. When he called the number again, it went straight to a recorded message and a softer, kinder version of the receptionist's voice. Mr. Mok was left wondering uneasily about the kind of place the old woman was staying in. *Well, I suppose I'll find out soon enough,* he thought. He made a mental note to call the following morning and schedule a visit for the weekend. That night, however, he received a call from his mother telling him that his Aunt Flora had died, and that the funeral rites would take place that Saturday and Sunday. Mr. Mok promptly gave his assurances that he would be there. He briefly considered visiting the old woman after his return, but remembered that it was generally considered bad luck to visit someone after a funeral. Or was that only for pregnant women and people with young children? Whatever the case, he decided he would have to postpone the visit. He spent the following weekend fishing with his father, who, as usual, chastised him for his poor technique, but didn't otherwise complain about his company.

When the weekend after that was almost upon him, his colleagues reminded him of the company softball game against the accounting and sales divisions. His division won, and a colleague whom he believed never thought much of him patted him on the back and said "Good game." The following week, the woman who'd stood him up several months previously invited him to a weekend away at her favorite hot springs resort. He learned that she had just split up with her boyfriend, and though he suspected that he would be little more than a distraction for her, he agreed to go anyway. The touch of another person, even without emotion, was better than nothing. And so it happened; one thing after another prevented him from arranging a visit to the old woman, and as his life became filled with more and more vaguely pleasing distractions, the thought of her began to grow ever more distant, and the cloud of stone that resided in his lungs seemed to lighten a little every day.

ACKNOWLEDGMENTS

Huge thanks to: Sunyoung Lee, for being a wise and brilliant editor; Neela Banerjee, for all the mountains you move; and everyone at Kaya Press, for your passion and hard work; Rachel Sherman, for your encouragement and guidance on the early drafts of this book; my writing buddies Rachel Khong, for the Ruby and our morning writing sessions at Charlie's, and Cathy Rose, for our evening writing sessions and France (I couldn't have finished this book without the both of you!); Chad Lawson, for making me write about what I didn't want to write about; Corinne Goria, Gravity Goldberg, and Gabrielle Ekedal, for your sister-friendship and for reading early versions of these stories; Peter Orner, Megan Camille Roy, Toni Mirosevich, and Micheline Marcom, for your wisdom and care; Alyson Sinclair; Sunra Thompson; and Maxine Hong Kingston, Gish Jen, and Peter Ho Davies, for letting me see myself in your writing when I most needed it.

Love and gratitude to my family: the Loks, the Lokabrasses, the Ayala-Loks, and especially Julien, my amazing and brilliant husband.

ABOUT THE AUTHOR

MIMI LOK is a Chinese writer and editor based in California. Born and raised in the UK, she holds an MFA in Creative Writing from San Francisco State University. She is the recipient of a Smithsonian Ingenuity Award and an Ylvisaker Award for Fiction, and her writing has been published or is forthcoming in *McSweeney's*, *Lucky Peach*, *Electric Literature*, *Nimrod*, *Hyphen*, and elsewhere. She is the cofounder and executive director of Voice of Witness, an award-winning nonprofit that amplifies marginalized voices through an oral history book series and a national education program.